STATIONS
of the **HEART**

STATIONS
of the **HEART**

STORIES

DARLENE MADOTT

EXILE
editions
fiction, poetry, translation, drama and nonfiction

Library and Archives Canada Cataloguing in Publication
Madott, Darlene
       Stations of the heart : stories / Darlene Madott.
ISBN 978-1-55096-262-8
I. Title.
PS8576.A335S73 2012   C813'.54   C2012-904785-6

Copyright © Darlene Madott, 2012
Design and Composition by Thank Heaven for Little Boys~mc
Typeset in Fairfield and Constantia fonts
Printed by Imprimerie Gauvin

Published by Exile Editions Ltd ~ www.ExileEditions.com
144483 Southgate Road 14 – GD, Holstein ON, N0G 2A0
Printed and Bound in Canada in 2012

The publisher would like to acknowledge the financial support of the
Canada Council for the Arts, the Government of Canada through the
Canada Book Fund (CBF), the Ontario Arts Council, and the Ontario
Media Development Corporation, for our publishing activities.

Any inquiries regarding publication rights, translation rights, or film rights
should be directed to: info@exileeditions.com

Canadian Sales: The Canadian Manda Group, 165 Dufferin Street,
Toronto ON M6K 3H6   www.mandagroup.com   416 516 0911

North American and International Distribution, and U.S. Sales:
Independent Publishers Group, 814 North Franklin Street,
Chicago IL 60610   www.ipgbook.com   toll free: 1 800 888 4741

This book is for special men, including Martin Teplitsky, O. Ont., Q.C., LSM, LL.D., who taught me as much about life as lawyering; Lad Rak, exacting better than my best; Brian Goldman, brother, about the business of life; Ricardo Federico, my other brother and professional colleague; Brian Hallahan, friend X 8; Filippo Isabella, inspiration to cycle; George Marnica, who exorcised my home, leaving enough spirit to keep me alert; Lorenzo Migliore, sensitive soul and Italian translator; Ercole Gaudioso, former NYPD and fellow writer; Jack (John) Razulis, first reader, fellow traveller and wine-maker; Dr. Brian McDermid, who told me I could visit him weekly or write; Timo Merio, man of the Malahat mist; Warren Giovannini, protector and love; Marcus, inspiration and wonder, from the day you were born; and

John Madott
(1918-2011)
father, artist at life and painting,
who taught me the best work is always the next.

Contents

Vivi's Florentine Scarf
1

Afternoon in a Garden of the Palazzo Barberini
20

Waiting (An Almost Love Story)
26

Getting Off So Lightly
58

"Solitary Man"
81

Open Sesame
104

Zachary and the Shaman
119

Château Stories
143

Powerful Novena of Childlike Confidence
162

Entering Sicily
177

Going Where, Exactly, With This Motion?
192

Travel Stories
196

Cycling in Sardegna
208

Acknowledgments
233

It is as if she were on a journey without me and I said, looking at my watch, "I wonder if she's at Euston now." But unless she is proceeding at sixty seconds a minute along this same timeline that we living people travel by, what does now mean? If the dead are not in time, or not in our sort of time, is there any clear difference, when we speak of them, between was and is and will be?

—C.S. Lewis, *A Grief Observed*

This, noble Sabinus, is but a stone, a very small token of a love as great as ours; I shall forever search for you. I ask only, if it be possible, down there among the departed – for my sake, do not drink of the waters of forgetfulness.[*]

—Anonymous (5th c. AD)
The Penguin Book of Greek Verse

[*] The epitaph to Sabinus in the original can move one to tears. Where I have rendered 'but a stone, a very small token,' the chaste Greek has only *he lithos* (the stone) *he mikre* (the small) and where I might have written "yearn for you" the Greek verb is actually "search for," "I shall search for you" and *aeei* (always) indeed imply a search for all eternity, since he does not give up hope of finding his beloved again, even though it be among the dead.

—I.F. Stone, "From the Greek," *The New York Times Review of Books,* February 22, 1979

VIVI'S FLORENTINE SCARF

Vivi put me up to buying the scarf at a marketplace in Florence. She was much older than me, nearly double my age, and my hesitation angered her. The scarf was bright, more of a sarong than a scarf.

"But what will I use it for?"

"Use? Why anything – to wrap yourself in, when you step out of the bath, *for your man*."

There was no man in my life. Single, I towelled down after a bath. I had learned from other students that Vivi was married to a rich German engineer, had four adult sons. She was travelling alone that summer, as were we all – studying *Quattrocento* art in Italy.

Vivi, dying of cancer, although undiagnosed, took the scarf from the market vendor and threw it about herself. The Florentine sun caught the gold threads between colours and the scarf transformed her.

"If you don't, I will."

Professor Lucke's first lecture (the only one in a classroom. All the rest were to be in churches, monasteries, graveyard chapels): "Why Tuscany? Why murals? Italy is the cradle of western civilization and Tuscany participates in this fruitful exercise. It is the nature of mural painting that promises to remain faithful to the original location of the image by the nature of the word 'mural' – wall. Wall painting needs a technique. *Fresco*. 'Fresh' – a technique where paint is applied to wet plaster. The pigment undergoes, by fact of wetness, a process of intense binding. The result is a painting of remarkable solidity, with the capacity to face the attacks of time. The mural, like love, is not transferable. It keeps us, holds us, wants our response. This art, it speaks to me. I cannot hear it. I just see the lips move. It is as if, through the ages, the sound gets lost. I try to find the bridge from here to there. I don't understand, because the language has been lost, like faith itself."

Professor Lucke tries to find a way back, to find it for himself. Every time he speaks to us, it is as if he is in intimate dialogue with himself.

Why Tuscany? Why murals? Does this answer for any one of us, his followers, why we are here? Why I am in Italy, the summer before I start my legal career? *I do not know what this thing is, my life.*

I do not know what purpose it has, what to make of it. To stay sane, study birds, study rocks, study anything. So I travel about Italy, carried by my own firm, slender limbs, studying the *Allegory of Obedience*, Giotto, Andrea del Sarto, Fra Bartolommeo, the upper and lower churches of Assisi, with the same searching intensity as I have studied law.

"Painting catches a moment. Prose flows like time. At a certain moment, Christ says, 'There is a Judas among us. There is one who will betray me.' Is this the moment the artist will choose, or the one when Christ first breaks bread, transforming it with meaning? What moment do you choose?"

"The thirties are the most awful time for a single woman," said Eva, the retired nurse. Eva had watched me talking to Branko, after class – Branko, who in Rome had told me about his anonymous encounters with men under bridges at night. "Life offers us nothing but a series of opportunities to feel ashamed." Branko would not put his arm around me at the Baths of Caracalla, when an open-air performance of *Tosca* turned cold. Shamelessly, I had asked him to hold me. On the bus back to Rome, I had told him how, at thirty-two, I still sometimes went home to my parents for a hug. He said, "You know, sometimes you make me feel very sad. I could give you a hug, but it wouldn't be honest."

As we walked down the stairs from class together, Branko told me about the man he had just met, about the dinner that continued with breakfast. Now the man was helping him find an apartment in Siena. Generous in his happiness, Branko gifted me with a consoling little hug. I wanted to smack him.

"In the thirties, a woman goes through an almost unbearable physical suffering, if she has no mate. It is the first time you realize you may never find one, and may never have a child. By forty, you have usually reconciled yourself to that thought. You don't suffer over it as much."

Eva had retired that year from nursing. She and I shared a bathroom at the *conservatori femminili* in Siena. There was a man Eva had loved in her late thirties, and who had wanted to marry her. He was ten years her junior. Whatever the reason, Eva made a decision against the man.

"Did you ever regret it?"

"No. It was not the man I regretted. I met him years later, and knew I had not made a mistake. It was the child." She said this matter-of-factly, as was her way, so that I almost missed it.

"You had a child?"

"No. *The child I never had.*"

Professor Lucke compares two paintings of the same subject – a Guido da Siena and a Duccio Madonna with child. In the first, both mother and child are preciously dressed, faces composed of geometrical forms. The child is less of a child than the visualization of an idea, our Saviour, who is our Saviour the moment he is born. In the Duccio, the child is a baby. Again mother holds the child in her left arm. But the baby has grasped a little bit of her cloak. Such a human gesture! You see the childlike playfulness of the gesture of her right hand – the way the mother holds those little feet. She holds a child's feet in her hands at the same moment she holds the feet of the crucified Christ. "Look at us and behold; we are human, he is human. You can come to me, because I am a mother. This is my little child. I know about you, because *I have gone through that.*"

The night before this lecture, I have a dream. I am in labour, the birth pains pulling me to earth like the force of gravity. It is not the pain of a menstrual period. It is as if someone has reached up inside me, taken hold of my womb, and is tearing me out – a cutting, annihilating pain. I wake on the single bed in my cell-like room, knowing my pregnant sister back in Canada must be in labour. I wake relieved that it is her and not me. For I am terrified of her pain. I do not want this cup for myself. Nor do I want to pass through life alone.

Coming back to the residence with Eva, I find the telegram and know, without opening it, my sister's child has come.

"Look and behold, we were human. He was human. You can come to me, because I am a mother and this is my little child. I know about you, because I have gone through that."

And I thought what he meant was the pain of childbirth. Never for a moment conceiving far worse. No, because in *this* painting, at *this* moment, mother holds the child's feet in her hands. *"Ah," said my son's eventual father, watching me play with the little feet of my only son, "You kiss those feet now. Don't you know those are the feet that will take him away from you?"*

She holds the child's feet in her hands, at the same moment as she holds the feet of the crucified Christ.

Vivi might be sixty-five, or fifty. She has been a model, has sold real estate, even taught – this in addition to having mothered four sons. Her pregnancies were terrible, with an overactive thyroid not diagnosed until she was in her late forties. She is Estonian – a tall, skinny blond woman, who does her makeup well, who dresses elegantly in melon-coloured silk dresses she made on her own – always womanly, with an innate artistry.

We met returning to the *conservatori femminili* late one afternoon. Recognizing each other from class, we went to Nannini's for tea. She seemed lonely, though in my ignorance I could not imagine how someone could be lonely in a life of such density. She said she had a decision to make about that night. Her taxi driver had asked her for a date. She was nervous about agreeing because her Italian was insufficient to lay the ground rules for the evening; on the other hand, she wanted to break out of the circle of females at our residence. I told her I wished for male company, too. I told her about Branko, and how it was frustrating to be frequently with a male who elicited female response, but had no male response. She said she really wished she could meet someone gay, that she loved gay men, they were so intuitive.

The next day in Florence, Vivi saw me with Branko and ran after us. She announced that she wanted to have a really good meal with people who looked as if they weren't afraid to spend some money. At lunch, we had two bottles of wine, were all a little drunk. Vivi talked and talked. At one point, she pretended to a weakness she did not have, and placed her hand on Branko's arm, as if for support. Branko preened at her touch.

"I do not believe you. You are a very strong woman," I said.

"You know that? I do not like the idea of being known."

On the bus that evening, we sat separate — Branko way in the back, Vivi behind me. At one point, I turned around to hear something Vivi was trying to tell me, and Branko caught my eye, behind Vivi's back, indicating with his hands the quacking gesture for talk, talk, talk. That he should thrive throughout lunch on her attention, only to mock her now, diminished him in my eyes, at the same time as he made me his accomplice. I decided to distance myself from them both.

The next day, Vivi wanted to return to the same restaurant. I said I did not like to repeat experiences, so Branko and Vivi dined that day alone. On the bus back to Siena, Branko surprised me, by taking the seat at my side. He told me Vivi had had a terrible earache; they had tried to phone some international alert for which her husband had bought insurance, and failing any contact, he had suggested Vivi sit down and relax and eat something first, and when she swallowed her soup, the thing blocking her inner ear seemed to burst, the pain dissolved, after which she felt fine. I thought Vivi's illness a ploy and was amazed that Branko had believed it.

Professor Lucke: "Monterchi. A graveyard chapel. Circa 1445. Piero della Francesca. Here we have a tent motif, the tent flaps parted by angels in a cere-monial way, so that we see the *Madonna del Parto*. This is not a common topic in Christian iconogra-phy – the pregnant Mary. You see the swelling of her body, hidden beneath a blue gown. Her feet are clearly visible. She turns slightly away from us. Her left hand on her haunch. Her right hand lies over a slit in her gown, a very soft, cautious touch; at the same time a gesture, which seems to point. This is a woman, in every sense of the word, expecting. Inside surface – padding – inside of a fur coat. Out-side a mantle. Promise of birth. Christ on the cross, promise of resurrection. Location, above the altar in a chapel of a graveyard. The meaning of the Euch-arist. She is the chalice that carries the Lord. Like the tent that shelters her, her gown shelters her body, her body shelters Him. Pomegranate. Euch-aristic symbol. Round and opened like her gown."

Professor Lucke is excited as he points, dancing in his running shoes, his eyes on fire with the symbols on the wall. His loose cotton shirt billows as sweat blossoms under each arm, with its pungent male odour, prompting Eva to comment, "He wants a woman," not in the carnal sense, but in the sense of a man wanting a woman to administer to the details, such as laundering his shirts.

I usually spent my weekends in Siena with Eva, lounging beside the Giardina pool. With Eva, there were no expectations, not even the necessity of conversation. We would sit side by side on our lawn chairs, observing the bathers from other countries from overtop our respective books, in parallel pursuit. Eva studied the course books in preparation for our final exam, while I read Boccaccio. Thus, in silent companionship, our eyes filled with the same images: there was this Swedish girl in a white bathing suit, translucent when wet, exposing her small breasts with their tight nipples, perched with a single bronzed foot coyly fishing the pool. Her young muscular mate swam up to her, lifted the foot from the water, and astonishingly, sucked her toe.

"Isn't she gorgeous?" was Eva's only comment. Eva was of an age – beyond surprise, beyond longing – accepting of seemingly everything. That day, and although Eva and I usually practiced our student economies, we ate at the Giardina restaurant. Without changing out of my black bathing suit, I wrapped Vivi's scarf about my waist, and waited in queenly composure for the barbequed rack of lamb to be brought to our table, treating Eva to wine. When supper was ended, I could not leave the bones on my plate. Wrapping them carefully in a napkin, I deposited them into my beach bag. Eva said nothing. Later, we laughed like complicit schoolgirls over the contemptuous silence of our Sienese waiter, removing my boneless plate. In the privacy of my cell-like room back at the *conservatori*, I gnawed upon my bones.

While I usually spent my weekends with Eva, one weekend I went to meet Vivi in Bologna. Our purpose was shopping. Vivi was taking me in hand. If I were to become a lawyer, I must dress the part. In Bologna, I would find Armani suits, and Bruno Magli shoes. Vivi knew just the stores, and the hotel across from the train station where we would each take a room.

I arrived before Vivi. Though discussed weeks before, we had not confirmed with each other before the designated weekend, and I was uncertain if she would, in fact, keep to the arrangement. Was it for this reason, or some other, that I made all my purchases without her? In the shoe store where I selected my shoes and bag, I told the saleswoman I would be practicing law on my return to Canada. "In these," she told me, "the Judges will not be able to resist your persuasions." For the black Armani suit, with buttons up the left leg of the skirt, I would find a tailored white and black shirt. I made my choices in an orgy of spending, all in one morning. Surrounded by a sea of tissue paper on the floor of my hotel room, I surveyed the purchases for which Vivi's approval had not been sought, and a wave of nausea overcame me. Was it the extravagance of what I had just done, or fear of my own choices?

At dinner, I told Vivi I had been about to leave Bologna. She burst into tears. Tonight was her birthday. I could not possibly know... What it was to have been abandoned by an alcoholic mother, a father unable to care for her, given into foster care. She had grown up thinking of the children who came and went as her brothers or sisters, never to see them again, never knowing when they would disappear. The father had thought he could get her back, had apparently tried – a fact not known to Vivi until the year after his death, when she had traced her birthparents and learned for the first time that she had been wanted by at least one of her lifegivers, that her father had tried. He had thought the Judgement temporary, not appreciating how in legal terms temporary can become final. There was one birthday; a man arrived at the door. She had been sent to her room, but not before she saw the shadow of the doll in his hands. They were delicate hands, with long fingers – the hands of a pianist. The doll had a porcelain head, later broken by one of Vivi's foster brothers. Now Vivi had a vast collection of dolls at her home in Canada, the home built for her by her German husband. She had four sons of her own. No, I could not imagine her sense of abandonment in Bologna.

"Duccio: We look into an interior, into something that could be part of a larger structure. Time here is convincing. People are joined together, having a meal – drinking, eating, talking, but lively. There is one in the centre. Again we have the motif of the one who leans against him. For sure, these people spoke Italian. We seem to hear them. Notice how much Duccio operates with hands, in contrast to Giotto, who seems even to hide hands. When shown at all, Giotto's hands are at rest. In Duccio, in proper perspective, the lines should converge on Christ. That would recede him. The way it is here, in the Duccio, the convergence point is outside the back wall. What principles did these people operate with? There is a construction, a syntax, an order that brings the disparate parts into a whole. Are these splinters of perspective renderings of observation, or constructions unidentified with external sight? We can't see this painting from Renaissance eyes. This is a way of seeing the world unknowable to modern eyes."

In Assisi, we dine together – Branko, Vivi, Professor Lucke and I – a rare night together, never to be repeated. Eva is bedridden, having eaten some tainted food. She takes her incontinence as a sign of demise, apologizes when I surprise her returning with some tea, to find her weeping alone in the dark. I had thought Eva beyond grieving, not understanding that one can always grieve one's own life. Eva, then, had been *afraid*. Alone in the darkness of our cave-like room in Assisi, Eva had been afraid.

That day, in Assisi, we learned from Professor Lucke of the Franciscans. "In the Franciscan spirit, there is the discovery of the individual, who has the capacity to judge, who in a sense needs to be converted." Like Professor Lucke, whose deepest need is to be converted – to believe, who arrives daily, a starved man at a banquet he cannot eat. It is easy for those who do, impossible for those who cannot. Faith cannot be willed. Like love. Neither for him, nor for me. "God is perfect. Man is imperfect. Whatever is imperfect, cannot be God. But Christ was born man. Yet he was a spiritual being, was not man. This must have been a deadly challenge to the Church, this Christian paradox. It meant in his very core God was man, born man, became man, lived like man, died like man."

Professor Lucke, Branko, Vivi and I eat together in an outdoor garden of arbours and vines. A guitarist from the nearby campground plays Neapolitan love songs. At outdoor kitchens carved into caves, there are large open hearths; we select our meals at the cave mouths. I have quail on a spit, cooked peppers and *rappini*. We bring Professor Lucke his favourite pasta, *con aglio e olio*. And of course, there is the wine!

In the arboured garden, Professor Lucke confesses to the problems of teaching in Italy, how people are overwrought, displaced from their sense of themselves, their normalcy. Branko repeats the

Tosca story I heard in Rome, about the transposition in the music signaling some epiphany in the plot. Professor Lucke tells Branko he likes opera because the music distances the emotion. He has this abstract thing to contemplate, interposed between himself and raw emotion. Vivi says it is only deep experience that makes life worth living. I sit distant and silent, wrapped in the scarf. My silence is wilful, for Branko has told me that afternoon that I am too caught in the vortex of myself, that I do not see people around me, the way they move away, as if from a fire, realizing that I know exactly what I want and, my God, I'm going to get it, and you better get out of my way until I'm done. "You are hard to be with."

Then, unexpectedly, Professor Lucke leans across the table and says into my silence: "This is a beautiful scarf." His thumb catches the fabric, like the scene of the lamentation with St. Francis outstretched, *and Girolamo, the one who could not believe; he catches the fabric and pulls it up and free of the wound and then pushes his fingers into the wound. We see him do that with terrific concentration. We see him from the back, kneel down in businesslike fashion, "I want to know," in contrast to everyone else, whose response is raw emotion.* Professor Lucke brings his face close to the scarf, and I can smell the sweat rise from his male body. Vivi smiles triumphantly. It is her taste he compliments; but *I* am the scarf. It is my beauty he means.

The next day, on a street in Assisi, he and I pass each other alone. Professor Lucke says he wanted to thank me for my company. "You," he says, "are very independent. One can see that immediately. Often, independent people drive away what they need."

Donatello's *The Conception*: "Yes, I will be the hand-maid of the Lord, and the very minute she gives her assent, she conceives. She hasn't here yet given her assent. Donatello focuses in on that moment, and gives it to us with a kind of dynamism. She doesn't say 'no'; she says 'yes,' but the conception only takes place when she says 'yes.' We know she will say 'yes' to conception, knowing of His impending sacrifice, as of her own. In this mural, it has not happened yet. This is the moment *before choice*."

It takes me more than twenty years to understand the gift of Vivi's scarf. By then, a middle-aged woman, with only one son to my flesh, I have an afternoon of love. I have emerged, damaged but not broken, from a failed marriage. To my surprise, there is a man in my life, enough years my junior to make me remember Eva. Remembering Eva, *I do not refuse*. We have all we can expect – a few hours on a Sunday afternoon between our respective obligations, the children's hockey games, the birthday parties. How shall I greet you? Wear nothing, he says, we haven't much time. But I cannot bring myself to open my door naked. It is not the fear of nakedness, but of my own imperfection – that he will see the scar of the caesarean section.

Vivi, I wrap myself in a vortex of colour. I stand behind my front door – a woman, in every sense of the word, *expecting*.

Ah, the delight of his eyes, when I open the door, of his hands, searching the colourful folds for an opening.

Vivi will return, that summer, to find a different colour of hair in her own hairbrush, left in the lavish master bathroom of her perfect home while she had gone to Florence to study art. Is it always thus, we discover ourselves betrayed? What choice did she have? The choice, only, of reaction. I was not there to witness. I will remember Vivi at the moment she threw the scarf in all its colours about herself under a Florentine sun. *If you don't, I will.*

Vivi, I do this in memory of you.

AFTERNOON IN A GARDEN OF THE PALAZZO BARBERINI

"È chiuso."

She stands in her khaki shorts, with her loose white blouse, its chaste suggestion of a sleeve slightly draped over the shoulders, her bare brown legs with the bobby socks and runners, her dark curls beneath a ball cap, and her knapsack, filled with research.

The Chief of Police tells one of his subjects to find out what *l'americana* wants at his gates?

"Non sono americana, sono canadese. È ben diver-so!" she declares impetuously, finding the words, she knows not where. But something in the way she makes this proclamation, slight stamp to the foot, almost-tears smarting her eyes, about having come all this way, with this squadron of men before and behind him watching the scene at the gate, must somehow have charmed him, for the Chief of Police smiles and approaches.

She has come all this way, from Canada, she explains from the other side of the gate, hands clutching the bars. She is searching for a painting by Artemisia Gentileschi, a *Cleopatra*. It exists here, in the Palazzo Barberini. Only here. Or so says the book. What the book does not say is that the Palazzo is closed, for renovations. *È chiuso.*

"*Ma non è possibile! Io non posso ritornare!*"

The *comandante*, taking pity, makes the order, and the gate opens. "*Non si preoccupi.* I show you a *galleria di dipinti.*"

He pats her on the head, on her ball cap, and she sees a look pass between two soldiers who are standing at the front of the line, on the ascending stairs, and she isn't certain what the look means but she follows after him.

He leaves his men on the stairs, escorts her across the courtyard and into the cool darkness of the Palazzo.

As they cross the first hallway, someone clips along at a rapid step and there appears a soldier, with a silver tray, with two glasses of Prosecco and the bottle. Her high-ranking escort stops the soldier, asks sharply where he's headed, confiscating the two glasses. He hands one deftly over to her. The soldier, flustered but powerless, clips off to a fate unknown but certainly unpleasant, given his confusion.

And so he opens a *galleria* with the huge set of keys at his belt, and begins his leisurely tour of the place. But not the painting she has come to see. She can barely conceal her disappointment. This is not the Artemisia painting. When will he take her to see the Artemisia? *Pazienza,* he counsels, always with this slight amusement about the lips. He shows her, instead, *The Rape of Lucretia,* and one seduction scene after another, and stands before each, displaying the artworks, not as an art historian, but as a voyeur, as a pander might, thinking to placate this *americana*. He is indulging her and, she realizes, she is also indulging him.

The small elevator is like a gilded cage. It is only when he closes the second ornamental door and they begin the ascent that she feels rising in her the panic of sudden comprehension. All unsuspecting, she has entered a trap. Her eyes meet his. He must read the fear in hers. She sees a slight embarrassment in his, before he looks away.

Moments later, they arrive, and he opens the series of cages and releases her with a flourish of an arm. He guides her toward a terrace, shaded by trees, and seats her at a white wrought-iron table. They are high above and hidden from the muted sounds of Rome. She sits and gazes into an elaborate boxed garden, with lemon trees and other shrubs she does not recognize, an established growth of many years, aromatic with herbs, full of gracious statuary, and a joyous sound. A yellow canary, not caged, but not fleeing either this internal paradise, sings in a tree not far from her. She is giddy with surprise and relief.

Grazie, she says to him and, reaching out, pats the hand he has authoritatively left on the table. He places his free hand over hers, as a soldier arrives. He breaks his hold to permit the soldier to spread the white linen, and then to lay the table with a modest repast of cheeses and fruits. The soldier manages to see nothing and everything. Again, it has simply and unexpectedly appeared. While the soldier does all this and places the bottle in an ice bucket, the *comandante* returns her smile, obviously pleased to be able to have this pleasure at his disposal and to be able to share it with her. He pours her another glass of Prosecco. He dismisses the soldier meaningfully, with a finality that indicates there are to be no further interruptions. She again feels an intense anxiety. After the soldier is gone, the old man makes his apologies. He is diabetic, and must eat simply. But she takes another meaning from his explanation, and after this, worries no more.

Although they have little language with which to communicate, he manages to convey to her that he has a ball to attend this evening, a gala event, at which there will be many dignitaries, and would she be willing to accompany him? Again, she touches the aged hand, this time to point coyly at his wedding band: "*Sei sposato,*" she says.

"*Non è importante.*"

"*Sì, è importante.*"

They both laugh. But she suspects he does not really expect her to say "yes" to his invitation.

She gives this to him: the silence of a single afternoon in her lifetime, full of the song of a single canary. Her *comandante* eats, as does she. Then her *comandante* dozes in the chair beside her, his hands folded across his stomach. She finishes the Prosecco, and turns the bottle, neck down into the floating ice. While he sleeps, she dips her fingertips into the ice bucket and takes the blessing onto her face and back of her neck, and feels the shard of ice melt down her back. She explores a little of the walled terraced garden, the object of which appears to be to exclude Rome, not see it, for there is no looking over these walls. Nor does she want to leave. Like the canary, flit she might, from here to there, but leave?

It does not even occur to her. Instead, she gives into this afternoon in her young life, with a stranger, asleep at her side.

After the siesta, the *comandante* escorts her down the staircase, where they first met, and she sees the men, lounging about the upper terrace, the landings, the courtyard, roused by curiosity at the spectacle of their leader emerging with the young *americana*. She understands. She understands completely. She was never at any risk. She turns back and kisses him on the mouth, briefly. Then she runs down the stairs, and pauses to wave and call back to him, looking only at him.

"*Grazie mille. Sei molto gentile. Sei magnifico!*"
And he smiles, every inch the *comandante*.
"*Sei magnifico.*"

Scan for the author reading this story,
or URL: www.tinyurl.com/ReadingAfternoon

WAITING
(AN ALMOST LOVE STORY)

When thou dost ask me blessing, I'll kneel down
And ask of thee forgiveness.
   —Shakespeare, *King Lear*

And grief still feels like fear. Perhaps, more
strictly, like suspense. Or like waiting; just hang-
ing about waiting for something to happen. It
gives life a permanently provisional feeling.
   —C.S. Lewis, *A Grief Observed*

They undressed in the dark, so he did not see her hands trembling. She said she had never made love to a man she didn't know. He said, probably not to one you knew, either. She imagined he laughed with his chin tucked into his chest – a shy laugh, or very guarded. At least he is intelligent, she thought. That made her feel less ashamed. She tried talking to herself. It was either now or never, the feeling in her stomach a kind of drowning.

"I don't want to get pregnant."

"Do you think I *want* to make you pregnant?"

She lay under him in a kind of panic, tried to deaden all feeling, to concentrate on something else, but the panic caught up with her. He withdrew without coming. She was almost grateful. Was he a kind man? Maybe. Maybe not. She asked if he was angry. He drew his hand down across his eyes and lower face, like a man after he shaves.

"It never is good the first time," he said. "Our bodies need more time to get acquainted."

Franny thought, I will not give you time. I will not let you touch me.

When he called the next morning, there was the fresh smell of cut sweet grass blowing through the open window. She told him she thought she was pregnant; she had been with her husband just the once before she'd left and they had made love. She said this to frighten him off, so that he would not trouble her again. Her lie drew him closer. He offered to help. It was not his problem, she said. He asked if she still loved her husband, if it would force her back to him if her fears turned out to be real?

But was any of it real? She remembered waking in the night to the panic of railcars being uncoupled and coupled. The train going nowhere. Waiting. Summer had turned into a kind of waiting. A waiting to return. A waiting to bleed. For she really did not get her period. Something had dried up in her.

They started off in the morning with breakfast at a restaurant overlooking the sea. Then he took her to the aquarium, where she saw for the first time beautiful coloured creatures that blossomed before her eyes like underwater fireworks. He told her their name – anemone – his eyes watching her lips as she repeated it. He never looked into her eyes.

Then he took her for a drive along the North Shore. He did not speak, and Franny lay back in the seat.

She had never known a more silent man. His silence angered her. She thought it willful, like the silence her husband had used to punish her. She resolved not to care. But she felt hostile. So she hit him with questions. What did he want from life? Who was he? What work did he do? What did he have to say for himself?

He said nothing. And then nothing. He was resolute about this silence of his. She felt flush with anger. She told him that his silence was like that of a peasant – without expectation. He looked at her in surprise, as if he were about to say something, but she saw him change his mind. So she lay back in the seat, resolved to forget about him. With the windows fully open and the air so warm, she dozed. They stopped twice. Once, to take a short walk into the rainforest, and then to explore a small fishing village where he bought her ice cream. By the time they arrived back in the evening, her face was burnt from the sun and sea air.

Hours after she had asked her questions and forgotten them, he told her his ambition had been to own one of those homes they had seen along the North Shore, to be a millionaire by thirty. He hadn't a doubt he could have done it. He told her that when he was a teenager he had bought a rowboat with a small motor, and had used to spend his Sundays gazing up at the cliffs, at the homes that looked, not down at him bobbing in the sea, but out at nothing, their windows as if blinded. A false dream. Like most desire, he said. He knew better at thirty. She wondered what had happened in his life to make him so devoid of expectation?

He ordered something not on the menu, something she had never tasted before – silken tofu in lotus leaf, with sliced shallot and enoki mushrooms.

As each dish came to their table, he served the food onto her plate, as if to make sure that she was eating enough, as if this were a long habit of his, to fill the plates of the people with whom he ate. She was charmed. The tofu tasted like air, like she was feeding on air. She touched his ankle with her sandaled foot. She told him she had not felt any hunger for days. He had given her back her appetite. He grasped her foot between his two and held it there.

Above the table, he never took her hand, hardly spoke. He looked always down, always away from her. She thought, he is not an easy man. He does not seem to need anything.

"Look at me," she said.

He would not look at her. She was sure his eyes were a pale blue, almost colourless. He reached down and put his warm hand around her foot, between the instep and the sandal. Then he gave the foot a tug, so that, like a bobbin on water, her body dipped down at the tug. She clutched the table for support and laughed like a schoolgirl at how silly that must have looked. His strange affection pleased her.

"I know nothing about you."

"What do you need to know?"

"Who you are, what you do."

He said, "You can't judge a man by what he does for a living."

She thought, then: it must be something that embarrasses him.

"You've told me nothing about your past."

He said he wanted to stop at a bakery before taking her home. He was going to buy her cakes for her breakfast the next morning. He had noticed she was too thin. He risked a glance in her direction and chuckled. She saw that she was right about his laugh, that he laughed inwardly with his chin tucked into his chest. She saw the pain she could cause with her questions.

"Why aren't you married?"

"I don't need a wife. I can do everything for myself." The directness of his answer made her laugh.

Was that all a wife meant?

Or was he giving her fair warning? Wasn't he saying they might be lovers, but he was not going to marry her?

At that she really laughed. Not to worry, she said. She had no designs upon him. In any case, she would be gone in a few months.

Franny let herself out of the car. She slammed the door. She did not take his box of pastries.

One day they met where the trolleys loop in Stanley Park and made the seven-mile walk around the seawall together. They had not brought their bathing suits or towels. At Second Beach, she lay back in the sand, overcome by the heat, and he half-sat, half-lay beside her, his hand under her head so that her long hair would not fill with sand.

He told her she was not pregnant. She did not have the look of a pregnant woman. Her body was just upset. It could be anything, he said – the journey out. He touched her stomach through her sundress and told her to stop worrying, there was nothing *in* there.

The dress she was wearing was a pale blue cotton with thin shoulder straps. It had a full skirt, and she loved the freedom of walking in it, loved the way the wind would catch it and wrap it around her legs. It was an old dress. She had bought it for her honeymoon. She lay on the sand, trying to remember why her husband had hated it.

Through the cotton, his hand felt warm and comforting – like the touch of a father. She put her hand over his hand to keep him there.

"What does a pregnant woman look like?" she asked. It sounded like a riddle, or the beginning of a joke.

"Half asleep," he said. "She has a stillness you do not possess, a cloud over the eyes, like a fish sleeping."

"How do you know what sleeping fish look like?"

"I know."

Franny showered and dressed in one of his shirts, and took the glass of wine he gave her. He kept white wine in his fridge, even though he himself didn't drink. He had made a resolution about drinking. It was one of those decisions about his life for which there was no explanation. The blinds were drawn, and the sun had turned the room brown through the slats. It was very hot in his room, the glass so cold; Franny drank from it.

They made love easily. She cried out when she came, and her cry startled him, for he stopped suddenly and asked if he was hurting her.

No, she managed, using the broken language of lovers.

He lay on his back in a softened mood. She saw bruise-like marks on his body. He told her he had once been a welder. He described the pain in his eyes whenever he had accidentally stared at the flame too long. It was a pain that came to life only hours later, would begin toward evening and increase steadily into the night. There was nothing he could do for it, he said, except cold tea bags. He always kept wet tea bags in his fridge.

Franny started to cry. Not for the pain, for his description of the pain – an insidious pain that only announced itself after the damage was done. He picked her up and carried her to a chair and sat with her on his knee.

"What will I do? What am I going to do?"

"With your life, you mean, or the next minute?"

"What will I do?"

He kissed her.

"Have you ever considered keeping your baby, if it turns out to be real?"

"Why do you want to be with me? I'm no fun to be with."

"I want to be with you," he said simply.

"Tell me what you most don't like about me."

"I like everything about you," he said.

"There must be something. My eyebrows? My voice?"

"I love your voice."

"My husband hated my voice."

There was a silence. It settled between them.

"Has it ever occurred to you that maybe you were never the woman he thought he wanted, that maybe he didn't know what he wanted?"

"It didn't have to turn out the way it did. I loved him, you know." She felt foolish, telling that to a lover.

He gave her a hug and patted her back.

"What will I do? What am I going to do?"

"Stay," he said, "and figure it out." He made her smile, then: "You want tea bags for those eyes?"

He became necessary. He was always there, someone else, someone with his own separate and impenetrable world. He asked nothing of her. There were the days she did not see him, and then the days she did. The days he said he could not see her, she imagined all sorts of things. She imagined he was a prisoner out on parole. The thought that he might once have done something violent frightened her, though she felt certain he would never hurt her.

"I didn't know until yesterday that I would miss you," she said to him one day.

They had rolled up their jeans and waded out to a rock off Second Beach to watch the setting sun. The incoming tide drew an ever-closer ring around them on the rock. Across the harbour, strings of coloured lights suddenly lit the masts of the tall ships moored there.

"Will you miss me when I'm gone?"

"I can take care of myself," he said.

"Can you?"

"Can *you*?" he answered, and she was startled by the edge in his voice.

Franny had spent the day earlier wandering around Chinatown, buying gifts for her family against her return. Sooner or later, she would have to return. She had just left a bakery carrying a box of assorted pastries when, across the street, she thought she'd seen him waiting for the light to change. He was with a woman. She started to run. She crushed the box of pastries against the old lady blocking her path. A horn screamed at the intersection. She grabbed his forearm and spun him around. There wasn't even a resemblance. She had to lean against a building to catch her breath, tears filling the whole moons of her eyes. She felt sickened. It had not even occurred to her that he might betray her in that way.

"I wasn't in Chinatown yesterday."

"I'm glad," she said. "You were with a woman."

"It isn't anything like that."

From across the water, they heard the low mournful whistle of a train. It was strangely beckoning. The tide was forcing them from their rock, which, anyway, had begun to grow cold.

"Is *he* what is forcing you back?" he asked, finally.

They always began their evening walks through districts that would remind her of her childhood, around corner stores and down laneways, where as a kid she might have hunted Popsicle sticks and pop bottles. They would end up in a restaurant, for he insisted on feeding her. This one had plastic grapes hanging from the ceiling along with last year's Christmas decorations. They decided on a pizza, while the owner went next door to buy the soft drinks they had ordered. They pumped the jukebox full of quarters and pressed buttons at random, laughing at Neapolitan love songs followed by Elvis Presley. Franny wanted to dance. There was no one else in the restaurant. But in this he would not oblige her. "Please," he said, looking alarmed, as she tried to pull him to his feet.

Midsummer night, they went swimming.

"You'll leave me suddenly," he said, "you'll leave me without warning. You won't leave me enough memories."

They had taken a shortcut through a schoolyard, their wet bathing suits rolled in the same towel. Lovers for three weeks, they were both three weeks behind on their laundry. When she'd told him, "I can't see you tonight, I have to do my laundry," he

had said, "Bring it over here, and we'll do it together." "Are you serious," she said, "my dirty underwear spinning around in there with yours?"

Their bathing suits would leave a humid little
patch on the wood bleacher when they were gone.
They sat together and gazed at the moon. She said,
"Let's plan to meet someday in Barcelona."

"We will never meet in Barcelona. One of us will
arrive too soon or too late, at the wrong corner, the
wrong night…"

He wanted to take her to the market. They
would buy a whole salmon and he would show her
how to make *gravlox*. If she could wait until late Au-
gust, they might take a holiday together. They could
hike into the mountains and pitch a tent beside a
lake, or he would rent a cabin if she preferred. There
were so many things still to do yet.

"You're not leaving me with enough memories.
We haven't made enough memories."

On the night of fireworks at English Bay, Franny had
a fever. For more than a week now she had been
waking with a weight on her chest, her throat con-
stricted and flaming. He listened to the symptoms,
and then he said, "You have homesickness. In your
mind, you are already leaving me." He wrapped her

in a sweater, even though it was July. He made a cup of tea and brought it out to her on the balcony, with two aspirins. She took the aspirins in her palm. They were very small and pink. She sat on the chair next to him, with her legs over his, watching the crowds converge toward the bay. He bent over and kissed her knees. He said he loved the smell of her knees, like two sweet flowers. Then he reached over and folded her in. He kissed her deeply. She did not want him to kiss her that way, because of her sore throat. She turned her mouth away. He crushed an aspirin and sprinkled its powder onto her tongue, stroked her neck as she swallowed. He kissed her again.

They made love quickly. He looked down to where she curled under him like a small burning animal. He just looked at her. "What?" she said. He just looked at her, as if memorizing her face.

Fireworks began exploding, shattering the warm blackness into a thousand stars. Each wave caught a glint of it and disbursed light, a handful of stars, so that they were surrounded by a galaxy. Franny felt as if two hands had taken hold of something in her chest and were squeezing it, ever so slightly. With each gentle pressure, she lost her breath. He held her. He held *onto* her, as if he were afraid she might slip under and drown; he might lose her in the black

space between lights. While she gazed up at the fireworks, he looked down at her face. "Oh, look," she
said. "Yes, look at you," he said. But the rest was lost
in a wonder of starbursts.

That night, he broke silence. Like the closed anemone, he suddenly opened. He told her he had a son.

"Why didn't you tell me sooner?"

"I am telling you now."

"Now is too late."

"I'm glad it's too late."

"It's as if you had lied to me. Why didn't you tell
me?"

"You were always going," he said. "I always knew
you would leave me in the end. There never seemed
to be any point."

"Why now, then? What has made the difference?"

He said nothing. He looked away. He looked like
a man condemned, waiting.

*What will you do, if it turns out to be real? Have
you ever considered keeping your baby?*

"Hold me," his child demands, whose father has
never asked anything of her, who makes no demands.

Franny makes an armchair of her body, in the shallow waters of English Bay, and lets her chin come to rest on his son's wet little shoulder, to see the waves as the child sees them, to see if he will let her – his dad's new friend, a stranger. What choice does he have? He is just four years old and this is his first time in the ocean, and she thinks what little courage he has to face the waves alone, how he paws the air behind him for her with his fierce little hands. Franny puts her arms around his waist and makes a shell of her body. From his height, the waves have been so huge and darkening, and for an hour now, have been too much. And he wants back to the shore, and once there he wants the ocean again, and when she gives the ocean back to him, he is sick on his excitement and yearns for the shore.

"Fickle," his father says, "like his mother."

"You shouldn't say that. He hears, you know. He will never forget."

"Kick," Franny shouts. "Kick hard and ride with it." The boy stiffens and pulls his little chest out of the water, hanging from her hands. Her back aches with his new weight. He shrieks ecstatically as he bicycles over the next wave, thinking he did it all on his own. Like his father. *Like his father.*

Throughout the afternoon, older women have smiled, and Franny smiles back, accepting a guilty maternity. There is a man on the shore – a man who knows, who has been watching her all afternoon.

"Why don't you take off your dark glasses and come in?" The child's questions give everything away. Franny is wearing a green and yellow kerchief wrapped around her hair, to match the green bathing suit. She keeps her head above the water.

"I am *in*, sweetheart."

"No you're not."

The child still has not looked at her.

For some reason, his father has not brought his bathing suit. Franny sends him back to the apartment to fetch it. His son's first swim in the ocean. This is too important to miss. They promise to wait the twenty minutes out on the sand. She will not let his son swim in the ocean. Together they will sit on this towel, she promises. She will teach the boy how to build sandcastles, while they wait for his father to come back.

The child kicks sand with his heel. He edges away from the towel, pushing the limits. There is no containing him. He is picking a wet string of seaweed from the sand and shaking it out like a tail. Anxiously, she seeks his father on the shore. The next moment a wave has flattened him, the boy who is more shocked than harmed, has only swallowed some water. She sweeps him up in her arms. His face has gone alarmingly blank, emptied almost, and then the whole weight of the day crests in a soul-shattering scream. She watches him turn red, little ribs pumping, face pulled into one convulsive knot. Just as suddenly, the sound stops, displaced by that unearthly stillness she finds so disturbing in his father.

"He's had enough," his father says. He stands beside them.

Franny is suddenly so tired she wants only to lie down, to curl up on the sand, to let the sun bake her.

"Tell me something," she says.

"Stay," he says, "don't go yet."

Franny leaves them shaking sand out of their towels, and walks to the women's change house. The man who has been watching her all afternoon looks up as she passes. He grins, as if to say, *I've got your number*. Franny stares at him murderously and the eyes slide away.

"Down, Daddy, please… please, Daddy."

They have caught up to her, the boy dressed hastily in a T-shirt and white sunhat, bouncing helplessly on his father's shoulders, clutching his dad's hair, while the father, slung with towels and running shoes and cameras and pants, secures him by an arm across the ankles. They look like a ship under full sail, the ropes and canvas not fully battened.

She touches his arm. The ship comes to rest.

"You don't like it up there, do you, sweetheart?"

"No." It is almost too quiet.

"So what do we do now? Would you both like some ice cream?"

"Let him down," Franny says. "He's miserable up there."

He lets the boy scramble down from his shoulders. The son stands apart from them, at an unforgiving little distance. Not a twitch. It is as if one move might draw attention to himself and land him right back up on his father's shoulders.

"So what do we do now?" the father says uncertainly.

Franny stares at the back of the little white sunhat, and presses her forehead with her palm. "I need shade," she says, "let's find a tree."

They are sitting on a park bench beneath the great outspreading branches of a tree, and Franny is so grateful for its green, for its solidity, she has an impulse to reach out and pat its bark. They sit facing the street. Bone-weary, is she, with an ache in her back that seems pulling her to earth. It suddenly occurs to her that the boy is not moving, not tugging at anything, not running off to be fetched back. He is just sitting there along with them, facing the street.

"You see that bus stop?" his father explains. "He thinks we're waiting for a bus."

Franny bursts out laughing.

"Do you mean that's all you have to do to get him to stay still? Find a bus stop and *pretend* to be waiting?"

She had been waiting for a bus when she met him. He'd had a cup of coffee in one hand, and had taken sips from a hole poked through the lid. He had looked relaxed, a newspaper tucked comfortably under an arm. She was furious at having just missed the bus, at the prospect of the wait. He had watched her pace. "You're from out of town," he had said. "After living on the coast for a while, you'll develop webbed feet. You won't take waiting so seriously."

"So what do we do now?"

Now, they were waiting. They were, all three of them, waiting. The boy was waiting for the bus. His father was waiting for Franny. And she was waiting for... something. She didn't know what.

"I have to buy my train ticket today."

The train station is like something in a dream. There are so many people, all trying to leave town, and nothing available on any of the days she thought to travel.

"I don't believe I am doing this," he says, as he dials the number for CN, the alternate route. For some reason Franny has not been able to get through; she keeps dialing the wrong number.

"Doesn't it tell you something?" he says, "Or aren't you listening?"

"So I'll get a ticket for the first available day, or I'll go by coach and not a sleeper. Nothing says I have to leave on a Saturday or Sunday, or any other day of the week. I have nothing to hold me."

He hangs up the phone and catches her. "Am I nothing?" As suddenly as the tears start, they have stopped. She wipes her face on his shirt and looks around for the son. The boy is keeping his usual respectful distance, his back to them both.

"Didn't even notice," she says, and laughs uncomfortably.

"Don't fool yourself," he says, "the little smartass sees everything."

An hour later, they come back to the spot where Franny has been waiting in line. The boy runs up to her, holding out his new rubber snake.

"And what do we have here, sweetheart?"

"We had hamburgers," the boy tells her.

"So is it done?" his father asks, grimly.

"Are you coming to Nanny's with us?" the boy asks, throttling his snake. She bends down at the knees and holds herself in a cannonball.

"If it's all the same to you, sweetheart, I think I'll wait outside on the sidewalk."

"Don't be silly," the father says, and grabs one hand from each. "How much time do I have?" he asks savagely. "How much time to change your mind?"

"It won't be changed," she tells him. "We have a week."

On the bus to Nanny's, Franny teaches the boy how to play "this-little-piggy-went-to-market," only his little piggies prefer spaghetti to roast beef.

"I didn't know you knew those kind of games," he says. "I never would have thought it of you." Franny wonders how he perceives her. He is sitting on the aisle seat, legs crossed, arm around them both, making a moon-curve of his body.

"I was a kid once, you know," Franny tells him. "I have a mother."

The boy's little fist bores into her stomach, supporting the whole of his window-gazing weight. She covers the fist with her hand.

To look at them, you might think they were a family coming home from the beach, sunburnt and spent.

"Where's his hat?" the father asks suddenly.

The child says nothing. His neck stiffens. Franny sees the blond hairs bristle above his sunburn.

"His mother bought it?" she asks.

"You know what this'll look like – like I haven't been watching, like I don't care…"

When they get off the bus, the child bolts in the direction of a grocery store. His father lets go of Franny's hand.

A woman is bent down beside a fruit stand, holding out a peeled banana, listening to what the child has to say. Whatever it is, he is telling it wildly. As they approach, the chatter stops. Her eyes move from the child to his father, and then to Franny.

"I've heard so much about you," she says. Franny is dismayed to think that while she knew nothing of this woman, her lover's mother has heard all about her.

"You are on holiday?" she asks. "Will you come back, do you think?"

"I don't know. At this stage in my life, I don't know that I want to repeat any experience."

"Even good ones?" the mother asks. She glances at her son, and in her glance Franny sees a mother's worry.

The child tugs at Franny's dress. He is trying to draw her away from the circle of adults, to tell her something. His little face is knotted with the effort. He takes her hand, and pulls her out into the yard. It seems his snake is caught up in the tree. As Franny reaches up into the branches, her stomach cramps with the unmistakable pain of her period.

It had been a masked pregnancy, he had married the boy's mother too young.

Franny asked what that meant – "masked pregnancy."

He said it happens when the mother denies to herself that she is pregnant, despite the growing signs. When his wife's labour had come, she was in a state of complete panic. It was as if she didn't know what was happening. She hadn't wanted to go to the hospital. She believed she had the stomach flu.

"I blame myself," he said. "I blame myself, for not really helping her."

Within a week of the birth, she had disappeared. She had checked herself out of the hospital, and taken the baby with her. It took him nine months to find the son – nine months of his son's life he knew nothing about. And then came the legal battles with the Children's Aid Society.

"What happened to her? What happened to your wife?"

"She committed suicide," he said quietly. "She was only nineteen."

That was all he would say.

He said he had known all along that Franny wasn't pregnant.

"How do you explain, then, the three-month absence of my period?"

"It was a false pregnancy. You wanted his baby. You still love him and don't know it. That's why you're going back."

Franny felt her face burn. She wanted to hit him. "That's not true," she said. "It's a lie." She hit him in the chest.

"You tell me," he said.

He planted a hand on either side of her and caged her within his arms. He forced her legs apart with his knee. She felt something turn over in her, a deep excitement between her ribs.

"Don't forget me," he said. "Don't forget you're coming back."

That night Franny had a dream. Her mother came to her by train. They met on a dark night, between cars. She held a box in her hands. Franny could not hear what her mother was trying to say to her. The squeal of metal drowned out the words. Lights flashed across her face. Her face was full of a mother's love, and something else – a strange new fear. They did not kiss or embrace. Their meeting was coldly unemotional. She had come all that way and Franny did not even kiss her. Her mother placed the box in her hands and sadly withdrew. Franny knew that in the box was her unborn baby.

On their last night, he took her to a Portuguese restaurant. It was called Le Fado. He told her that a *fado* is a sad song a sailor sings for his country, missing his home.

"You made my summer," he said. "I know this hasn't been a very good summer for you."

He was sitting back in his chair, a little distant from her. His arms were folded across his chest. His body looked relaxed. The body of her lover. Strong and quiet. He was letting her go.

It was the first time he dreamt of her, he said – a sign that in a way she had already left. In his dream, a tree was burning in the corner of the living room. It was burning from inside. He could see this through a fissure in its bark. He took a sheet from his bed and began to wrap it around the trunk, thinking to smother the flames. But as he bound the tree, he felt the heat grow fiercer. He had to unwind the sheet to take a second look. Through the crack, he saw flames turning the whole inside to white ash. It must have been burning like that for the longest time. He realized he would have to take an axe and cut through to where it burned, to put it out from inside. But how could he, without felling the whole tree? He had understood, then, he could do nothing for the tree.

"I woke knowing the fire was your love for him, and that you, somehow, were the tree."

He took Franny's hand. He turned it over and laid a kiss in the palm. He looked down at the palm and touched it with his fingers, as if to see if his kiss had left any impression.

"You don't have a lifeline," he said, looking up at her in surprise.

"That's ridiculous," she said, "I'm here, aren't I?"

"Are you, Franny? Were you ever here? Sometimes your love felt like something I intercepted."

Franny looked away. She felt ashamed. She had wanted him to love her, *needed* it, selfishly, for herself – to cancel out that another had not. She felt responsible for this.

"Once," she began, "I sat in on one of his math classes. He taught at the university. I wanted to surprise him, to watch him at his work. For a whole hour we were in the same room together, without his ever once seeing me. When the class was over I went up to him. I stood among the students near his desk. He looked right at me, without seeing me, as if I weren't there. Did it happen, I wonder? Or was it just something I imagined? It made my whole life seem tenuous."

He shifted in his seat, imagining her there, seeing her face waiting to surprise another man.

"When I left him, he never called. Not even once. Not even to ask why. It was as if we had never been married. I lied to you about that, about seeing him before I left. I didn't have to run away. He would never have come after me... Don't hate me," she said finally, "I have to go home."

Silence. His low voice. "I know," he said.

"I just wanted you to know."

They agreed not to have any trainstation parting. They agreed not to write. "There must be some reality to our relationship," he said. But no sooner was she tasting prairie dust than she had written her first letter, and there was a letter waiting for her when she got home:

"It has been two days since I saw you and it seems as if you are just around the corner some-where, but I just haven't stumbled around that right corner yet. It's a feeling of helplessness. You were here, and then gone, and nothing is the same since you left. Today, riding on the bus down Hastings past your old stop, there was a girl walking – slender, with long hair swinging down her back. It embar-rasses me to say that my heart skipped a beat. I almost choked. Back to my senses before the bus passed, I strained to see her face. She was nothing like you. Do I see you everywhere? Or is it, as I fear, that I am already forgetting? And when *will* I see you again? For I must see you again, Franny. I must…"

She had wanted to comfort him: "There was this corner, where I stood, not long after my return to the east, waiting for the light to change." What hap-pened there? It had changed. It had changed again, and still Franny had stood, not crossing the street. Then she had stepped sideways and into a phone booth. She hadn't answered his *hello,* listening instead to the voice of a wailing baby in his background. *He has a child – already,* she had thought, of the husband who had not sought after her, who had not waited for her return. It was as if she had been waiting on that corner, forever, while he had gone on and was miles and miles ahead of her. *And now you are behind me,* she had wanted to tell him, her man of the west, but did not. *Now I know that waiting is a kind of grieving. It comes before the thing you are waiting to die is actually dead.* She had stepped out of the booth and off that corner.

The letters that followed were constant in their tone. They were even, and tender, and wise. A new voice had begun to emerge in them. He spoke of things with wry humour. Whenever Franny read his letters she thought of his laugh, the way he had laughed with his chin tucked into his chest. This was not that laughter.

They were two months into writing letters when he said he was coming east. He would be whatever she wanted. He would be lover, or husband, or friend. She had only to say the word. But Franny was afraid. *And what if I say "yes" and he doesn't come? What if these are only words, in a letter? And if the words were truly meant, why wouldn't he simply show up?* She wrote and asked him not to come.

A year went by without a letter. When she wrote again, it was a few words on a Christmas card. With what joy she found the letter that followed in her mail slot. In the letter, he spoke of a journey he had made with his son, "the little squirt, now grown into a back-talking little prick," he wrote with fatherly affection. They had "cruised across country" in one of the wide-tracking Pontiacs he said he was "wheeling about with these days." He had taken his son back to see the hospital where he had been born. Franny understood that her lover was making peace with his past, with a young mother's suicide, with himself, was leaving all this behind, back where it belonged, a long time ago, now. She felt a fierce surge of release, not so much of freedom but escape, and at the same time, seared to the core by an almost sexual grief, as when he withdrew that first time, without ever coming. Surely she had never been so wondrously, so almost in love.

On her knees before the raised hearth of the sunken living room where now she lives, she is on her knees, cleaning out ashes with a bronze fire iron. As Franny reaches to remove one log's remains, she feels a hot pain from palm to heart. *Did I let it die, or did you let me go? And why is it that we did that?* She sees his eyes, bleached by the acetylene flames of fabrication, the eyes of her almost love, alone in the shop where he fabricates, alone and still waiting. *Forgive me, as I forgive you.* Palms to forehead, her eyes closed, impressed now with ashes, she sits back on her haunches, before the fireplace, where last night she had stared at the flames too long, unable to move. She presses down hard against her closed eyes until veins of light explode in the darkness behind her lids. Then she releases her palms, gets up off her knees, and goes...

GETTING OFF
SO LIGHTLY

She sits in the passenger seat beside her husband, Zachary. She is pregnant for the second time. Her first miscarried. She and Zachary weren't married at the time of the miscarriage. She had agreed to marry Zachary only after she'd learned that she was pregnant. A few weeks before the wedding, the miscarriage happened. In the hospital, Zachary had placed his bald head in her lap and wept into her hospital gown. He had said of the lost baby: "At least our dear little one got us together. We made a commitment to each other. We bought a house." She heard his unspoken fear – now that the child was lost, she would be too. Moved to pity by the tears of the man weeping into her lap, she responded to his pain: "Don't despair, I will have your baby, one day."

They are driving now toward the corner of Hastings and Main in Vancouver, where another man waits for her under a clock.

In the letter she wrote to this other man four months ago, she said: "I will be travelling to Vancouver with my husband, and I have already discussed with him the fact that I would like to see you again. I will understand if, for whatever reason, *you* do not wish to see *me*."

That morning, she had asked Zachary to let her off a block early, not wanting to meet the other man again under Zachary's eyes. Zachary promised. But he drives now right up to the corner. As she gets out of the car, she looks not toward the man she is going to meet, but back to the car. She sees her husband scanning the sidewalk for the man who might fit her descriptions. She refuses herself to look for the man, to lead Zachary to him. Instead, she stands on the corner, arms crossed, cheeks flushed with anger, willing Zachary to drive away. Only when the car pulls out from the curb and back into traffic do her eyes find him.

He leans against the wall, in a lineup of men who are always leaning against the wall, making no move to come forward, to single himself out. She knew she could count on him. He is looking past her to the car. She supposes he is thinking: "So that's the man you chose. Did he come to you, dick first, or use a more indirect approach?" This man who had told her years ago, "Be careful. Men will figure you for a catch, a woman who can take care of herself, who carries herself like a crab with its shell on its back." Had she not known he too was a crab, she might have thought the warning included himself.

This man, she had loved. Who would not marry her. Not anyone. What need of a wife when he could do everything for himself? He had told her this before she had known he'd had a wife, once, and a child, had himself raised the child with the help of a mother who took the boy between sea voyages. Part of her believed he'd only said this about not needing a wife to protect himself against need. She was one year into her law practice when he came east to visit her. They were driving through downtown Toronto when she said: "I want a house like that." He stopped the car, and backed up, surprising her with his interest in any house. It was an old townhouse, with a caged tree surrounded by interlocking brick. She liked the narrow, courtyard feel amid the density of city living. Shyly, she had asked him, "Would you live with me here, if I bought a house like that?" His only answer was a sort of snorting laugh. How ridiculous the question had been. She saw him standing solitary on the deck of his ship, his grey eyes staring out toward a night sea – feeling wind, feeling solitude – his own balance set against nothing. He would never live with her in her city house, the one she did eventually buy with her own money.

"Your letter said you had cut it." He sees her indirectly, his eyes circling her hair. "I'm glad to see it's still long." He has this way of taking in a thing whole, by casting his eyes about it, like a net. He hasn't noticed yet that she is pregnant.

She got pregnant on her birthday. Zachary woke her up singing with that boyish playfulness of his she thought would one day make him such a good father:

Happy birthday to you,
You live in a zoo,
With the elephants and the monkeys,
And I love you.

She had thought: he wants a child. He had not said a word about it since the miscarriage. If truth were told, the miscarriage had been a relief. She was afraid to have a child. Zachary knew that too. He had told her if it came to a choice between never having children and having her, he would chose her. That morning of her thirty-seventh birthday, hearing Zachary sing, she had changed her mind, despite the fear.

She looks up at the clock.

"Zachary is picking me up back here in a couple of hours. We're taking the 2:30 ferry to Victoria."

"I'll take you down to the quay. We'll walk some shoreline."

At four months, she doesn't really show yet. She is wearing a blue-jean dress – the one that hugs her torso and hips, then furls out in a long, full skirt. She wears it with a low-slung, country-and-western-style belt, studded with fake gems. City casual. City slick.

They walk in silence. And then he says, "You haven't gained any weight." He says it approvingly. She wondered if he would know. Years ago:

"You don't *look* like a pregnant woman."

"What does a pregnant woman look like?"

"Like a sleeping fish," was his answer.

Don't I look like a sleeping fish? It is on the tip of her tongue to ask, now, as he says:

"You look grand."

She is suddenly so grateful to him, she wants to weep. What is it about this man that always melts her heart? Is it because he loved her at a time when she was so unlovable – for no reason at all – like sending her the dozen roses the day before she married Zachary. *Love always*, he had said in the note. Simple. Inexplicable. Love always. Yet she had no doubt it was true.

She keeps silent. This is not the way she wants to tell him.

They come to some train tracks. They are out of the seedy part of town and into an area where there seems to be no one, just storage shacks, landfill and weeds. It is ugly, desolate. Where is he taking her? Why has he brought her here?

She is suddenly gripped with fear. For herself. For that other one – the life inside her. The same fear she used to feel so often when they first met. Fear of him, of his silence. *Who are you? Where are you from? Where are you going? I am myself, alone. I am what you see.* And what did she see? With that fish vision of hers, seeing always from the sides of her head. She had seen all sorts of things – a criminal, perhaps a murderer, someone running from a past, someone who would not unlock the storehouse of his memory, nor reveal himself, no matter how hard she tried. No amount of cross-examination would avail. She had feared him. And yet with this fear, she had given herself to him, over and over again. Because she had wanted to die. At least part of her had wanted to die. The other part left notes in her wallet, on her telephone message pad – places the police might look if she went missing. She would rip up the notes on returning home safely, only to remake them again the next time, when he called her days or weeks later. Where had he been? No answer. They could talk about their past together, the past they were creating. The past they created over the next ten years. And what they wrote to each other, the scenes they painted in each other's minds, became as real as the moments together, for those engraved images upon their imaginations that grew over time. So he had been with her on holiday to Avignon, brushing her long hair at an open window, shooing a pigeon away with the back of her brush; and she had been with him on board his commercial trawler, playing chess with some mate, watching islands approach like ghosts from the mist.

And when he came east to her city, the first time she would let him visit her in her city, she had trembled as if from some bitter cold, as she told him how very close she had come to *that*. She had lowered her voice and grit her teeth lest someone in the restaurant hear her blasphemy – how there had been a time when she had so hated her life that... That was the one time he had looked at her directly, taking her hand, gripping her with his eyes: "You must never do *that*. *That* is not the way you will leave me." Then he had counselled: "To stay sane, study birds, study fish, study anything." So she had decided to study law.

"Did he walk toward you, prong forward, as in a game of blind man's bluff? Or did you again orchestrate the affair, making sure *that he too fell in love with you?*"

If the truth were told, she had been dying from loneliness, for the want of someone to love.

But apart from their beginning, when – for the space of one summer – she had lived in his city, they'd seen each other rarely. She would not return to the west. He could not move inland, away from his port city. In the meantime, he raised his son; she went to law school. She began a career that committed her to staying put.

"I am honestly pleased to know you are happy, as you could not have been with me: crazier than a March rabbit, and woollier than a coyote, prick avowedly polygamous. I saw that I could never offer you what you desired…"

He has gone ahead of her, down a small incline beside the train track. Feeling her not beside him, he turns around, assesses her hesitation, and then holds out his hand. She takes it. It is the first time this day they have touched – a non touch – not like the solid grip of their past. He guides her over the rocks and landfill, down toward the shore, the two of them looking not at each other, but down at her shoes – the delicate, white lace-ups with their thin soles she had polished this very morning, while Zachary had watched her grimly over his coffee and had promised to let her off a block early.

"There is always the risk, with this type of thing, that you might meet someone else," he had said to her on one of his last visits to her city.

"What would you do?" she had asked him.

"I would be heart broken," he had said.

"Would you fight for me?"

"I would not fight for you."

That he would not fight for what he wanted, that he could give her up so easily, made her angry.

"I don't suppose there's any point in asking if you would still see me this way?"

"No," she had answered without hesitation. "I would never do that."

"I didn't think so."

"I'm not that sort of woman. I know who I am. I would never do that to any man I married."

"I didn't think so."

They had made love that night, as if for the last time. Every time they made love, it was as if for the last time. It was spring and she had left the windows open. It had rained all day and the air was fresh with the smell of worms, the sound of cars passing on a wet city street. They had made love and part of her had died with him again, as it did every time. Afterward, she'd lain under him like a crushed animal. He'd stroked her face, very gently, with the back of his hand.

"What?" she'd said, looking up at him, at his eyes glistening down at her in the dark.

"It kills me to think of you making love like this to any other man."

"I never will."

"Never say never," he had said. "We never know what we might do."

"I *know*," she had answered the man with confidence, "I know who I am."

So he'd known, when she wrote to him about Zachary, that it was over for them.

"Something has happened," she wrote. "Although we have not corresponded in over a year, I feel I owe you the knowledge."

She told him about Zachary, typing up her description of him as if she were setting out his qualifications for a job. "Zachary is a real estate and corporate lawyer," she began. "He is also an avid gardener. He has just gone outside in the autumn rain, pushing a wheelbarrow with a rhododendron for transplanting to the front of our house. (We had the front garden terraced this fall, with a lot of stonework.) He has grown his winter beard. I admit to loving him more with his beard than without it. I am sitting at my kitchen table as I write this, looking out at the backyard through the solarium. It is there he will start his seed trays in the winter for the spring plant. I feel such gratitude to him, watching him go by with the wheelbarrow, intent upon his gardening, totally unaware of the betrayal in his wife's quick little fingers."

In the same letter, she told him about having cut off her long hair. She told him about her new house in an established neighborhood, with its great maple tree in the back, how she loved that tree, had wrapped her arms half around it the day they moved in. "There is something else," she continued, "... Although I thought I never wanted a child, the moment I learned I had conceived, I began to love the life growing in me. The loss of it was one of the hardest I have ever had to bear. Perhaps this is why

I am telling it to you, to whom I have always been able to tell everything."

She and Zachary had married three weeks after the miscarriage. It seemed that with the loss of that child she had fallen in love with Zachary, who had not hesitated for a moment when she told him, who had blushed with pleasure and gone hard against her.

That was over three years ago, now. The cut roses had arrived the morning before the wedding, with their simple note: *Love always.*

He had not fought for her. And she'd had no doubt that she had broken his heart.

They are standing now on a dock, which juts past the ramshackle buildings out into the bay.

"On a weekday, this place is buzzing. I buy my fresh fish over there."

"We're renovating the house. We're doing over the basement, making it into a flat." She leaves out the word "nanny."

"Of course," he says simply, as if renovations were a foregone conclusion.

They look at each other and laugh. They laugh and laugh. His laughter reaches out and forgives her.

It's all right, this laughter says, to want something so ordinary, to care about your floor tiles and the colour of your walls.

"You'll be fine," he says. "You look happy. Marriage obviously becomes you. You must have needed to be married."

She wants to hit him for that.

"Did you ever mean it, when you told me you were going to move east?"

"Yes," he says simply.

"You never would have come."

"Wouldn't I?"

"We'll never know, will we?"

But he has said what she needed to hear, possibly what she came to hear. I did not betray you, your conviction of who I was, what we were. It didn't come together as we hoped. It doesn't mean I didn't love you.

"Having returned from a remote part of Pacific Rim National Park – a stay that started early July following my layoff – I realized I could no longer proceed according to the earlier plan." That was how he had started his last letter to her. Was that supposed to explain it – the months of silence, after she had finally said "yes" – a process that had taken ten years? Ten years, while she had gone to law school, while his son had grown up, ten years to realize that the back-and-forths were not enough, that she loved him, that she wanted to be married. "… I have rented a place and prepared for spending another winter here. It follows that my plans have been delayed, not changed. I do not presume that you will see it that way. I thought of returning the keys to your apartment in person. However, the prospect of arriving with bad news and who knows what kind of departure kept me from doing that. For that matter, I would rather that you came out west again for a change, if you will consider it anymore at this stage."

Coward, she had thought. Consider it? It was out of the question. She wrote back sharply:

"Your silence of almost two months prepared me for the disappointment contained in your last letter. It did not come as a surprise. What surprised me was that you could have deferred, until the last moment, telling me what you yourself must have known back in early July, when you say you were 'laid off.' I will not spend the fall as I spent this summer. I will not let you turn me bitter over what has been between us, nor give you the chance to make me regret ever having met you. I am ending this now."

And end it she did. Determined woman that she was. She went out and met Zachary. That very November. It wasn't until Christmas that he'd let her "jump his bones," as he put it. She did not "orchestrate their affair." Zachary knew her game. He was not going to let her get off so lightly.

Zachary. Who did not let her down. Who had flushed with pleasure and become hard when she had asked him, "What does it feel like to hold a pregnant woman?" Words that sounded like the beginning of a riddle or a joke. Zachary.

"What do you want from life," she had asked him when she first met him. "That's easy," Zachary said, "What everyone wants," he had answered.

"What is that?" she pressed. Was she finally going to have an answer?

"To be happy. To be rich."

He said this without irony, with the most uncomplicated grin.

"What do you want from life," she had asked that other man, over ten years ago. He had said nothing. They were hiking together. They had come to a mountain lake and had surprised two lovers lying naked on a rock. He looked across the lake as the lovers scrambled for their tent. He said nothing.

She'd grown impatient. Finally, he had laughed – whether at the question or the sight of the lovers, she never knew which. Later that afternoon, he had taken her standing with her back against a tree – his need so urgent, so pressing, it carved the tree into her back. "I used to want to be rich. I had this stupid dream to be a millionaire by thirty. That's before I learned the futility of all desire."

"You're a coward," she had accused. "Isn't it easier not to want, so much easier than to risk losing? How does one live without desire?" She had not believed him – that it was possible to make love like that without passion. And once to have had it, to be able to let go. *I will not fight for you.*

She had looked at Zachary, with his simple grin. He wants to be happy. He wants to be rich. What would it be like to attach one's life to such a man, to want such simple things? To get through life in baby steps, one choice at a time – like, what colour to paint the kitchen walls?

Zachary wanted a child. Zachary wanted her.

She thought the two irreconcilable.

"Marry someone younger," she had told him. "Some women are mother material. I am not." Hadn't she known that about herself since the age of fifteen, watching a movie about childbirth in the medical pavilion at Expo 67, seeing the pulse of blood gush from between a woman's spread legs, the afterbirth? Not me, she had thought, *never me.*

Never say never. We never know what we might do.

The day the bleeding started, she had a court appearance out of town. All the way to Milton and back in a mounting snowstorm, she had thought: *I am losing my baby. I am losing it because of this, because of people whose lives are not my life, who are nothing to me.*

After court, she had gone to see a friend. Throughout the afternoon, she had lain on the friend's couch, holding her cup of tea. She wanted so badly just to stay still there in the friend's house, her hands around the cup, the cup in her lap. Her eyes closed and she fell asleep. She woke to find the friend had removed the cup and wrapped a blanket around her lap, did not seem to mind that she had fallen asleep in the midst of her story about the kids...

Never say never. You never know what you might do.

The next day, Zachary came to pick her up at the hospital. "Why didn't you call me? You're such a strong woman," he said, "to go through that alone." She felt his unspoken fear, that she would leave him,

74

now there was no reason to stay. He kneeled before her and put his head into her lap. While his sobs wet through her hospital gown, she stroked the bald dome of Zachary's head. Zachary wanted a baby. He wanted her. He knew so simply what he wanted. Wasn't it easier to give Zachary what he wanted than to know it herself? At least to give Zachary what he wanted was within reach.

The sun comes out – after weeks, apparently, of rain.

"You brought the sun with you."

They are walking back toward town in search of coffee.

"Let's sit outside. We get so little sun on the coast." He borrows a cloth from the waiter and wipes off two chairs and the table.

"Have you never felt alone – so alone you think you will die?"

Silence, as he considers.

"Motion helps. Wind in my face. I usually enjoy the journey."

She will tell him, eventually. She will announce the birth of her son in a Christmas card – the son with whom she was pregnant that afternoon in Vancouver, that afternoon she went forward to track her past.

"... Sundays were the worst. Yet for all the loneliness I felt when I met Zachary, I used to insist on those days alone, apart from him. And Zachary always gave them to me. Without any resentment. The odd thing is, Zachary also had this independence from me. For example, when I had my son, I didn't have to worry about Zachary. He knew he had been completely eclipsed and just accepted it: as long as I was happy with my baby, it was fine by him that he was excluded from our orbit. I will always be grateful to him for that."

The man wrote back:

"... I've taken to driving a motorcycle. Even in foul weather I do feel the urge, put on my Black Diamonds and steam my way through the Malahat mist, riding past midnight into the little hours. Summers I push it, seeing how much it can do, but the speedometer possibilities are, as usual, lies. On the flat, even downhill at full torque it won't do much over one hundred miles. It does stand up on its back tire from a start, but I don't know how to do the trick very well; and the effort almost scares the shit out of me – and that, believe it or not, is cause for delight.

"The same bike has taken me 'off' the highway, although it is a street version. (It sat in my townhouse living room as the chrome conversation piece for the first winter.) But it went slip sliding on logging roads similar to which I was used to driving in earlier years; and it came out buzzing like a chocolate-coated insect. I drove it down long dry washouts and ran it across a small river. The machine is five or six hundred pounds, so partway success on that obstacle was not possible. In fact I was surprised that it did not tilt midstream because it had kind of flipped around on some muddy trails elsewhere.

"On such occasions, feeling momentary euphoria because of so-called success with the bike riding, and because the experience is a wonderful mix of reality and fantasy, it is easy to ask: 'Is this *it?*' Equally easy for another, not involved, to quickly answer no, life is not about euphoria achieved in overcoming obstacles. Although I think of such things, the 'it' question does not organically come to me since I went to the beach. I think I mentioned to you at our last meeting, I spend weeks there, literally, and see no one. No footsteps over a mile and

a half of sand for days. There, having often forgotten
what day it is, or even forgotten to rate days in the
abstract, that is apart from foggy, rainy, windy, cold,
warm or hot; there, I have known that *it* is *it*,
although I would not want to say it seriously, for fear
of spoiling it.

"From the above you know that I have not
worked for hire much. I taught again, hated it much
worse than before, and quit. Still thinking about
working in the food industry, but more likely I'll do
my own. I've been developing a herring pickle. Like
reinventing the wheel you might say, but mine is
better. The point I would make is my needs are little. For instance, sailing. Need or extravagance?
Anyway, my neighbour on the little island, who is in
The Guinness Book of Records for sailing around the
world solo or some such thing and *who owes me*, will
be coerced into taking me aboard the famous cir-
cumnavigating vessel he keeps at Thieves Bay.
Furthermore, my sort of buddy who works on the
big island at a peeler bar as the tap man *promised* me
the use of his fishing vessel moored at the quay. My
investment – rods, gear, mostly stuff I got for the
Steelhead run in Stamp River earlier. Small needs.
Might have to get a freezer though, and a wheelbarrow to cart the salmon from the dockside to the
house.

"Now for *more* of *what you did not ask about*. I fell in love once again, but it did not last. Never does, only the kids do. Speaking of kids, that is one sweet-looking boy in the photo. Hope you're not too busy to spend more than just 'quality time' with your son. Worst thing for people like you and me is to nanny them off. I guess that's because, among other things, we are people 'of the head,' meaning we have to, we just *have to know*. And what is there to know? Who we are going to live with (presumably) for the rest of our lives, what they are about…"

She is heading back toward a corner – "… the corner of Hastings and Main, in Vancouver, where I will meet you. Under the clock…"

"Will you meet my husband? We could go to lunch together. He is a good man, Zachary. I think you would like him."

"You're not going to make me go through that, are you?" he asks gently, without looking at her, looking over her, catching her whole in the net of his eyes.

"No," she says, "I won't ask." She knows if she did, he would oblige her.

"But if you want a good restaurant…" and he tells her about this little hole-in-the-wall that serves up succulent fried oysters.

Zachary and she go there. But the oysters are a mistake.

They do catch the 2:30 ferry. On the way to Victoria, she is sick to her stomach. Motion does not help. When she emerges from the bathroom, limp from throwing up, there are tears in her eyes. Through her tears, she sees Zachary out near the railing. He is looking out to sea. Unexpectedly, he turns and finds her, as if by instinct, like the needle of a compass finding north. The smile he gives her is one of pure delight. She is so grateful to him, for this smile. Her recent husband. She rushes to join him. Pregnant again, she is – this time by choice.

Zachary ropes an arm around her and kisses her eyes. Misinterpreting their moisture, he says gently, "Did you really think you'd be getting off so lightly?"

"SOLITARY MAN"

Don't know that I will but until I can find me
A girl who'll stay and won't play games behind me
I'll be what I am
A solitary man
A solitary man
> —Johnny Cash lyrics to "Solitary Man"

Earlier that year Francesca had told her husband, if he cared about her and their son, he would book a holiday for them; he would pay for it and take them away so they could finally be a family together. She had only two weeks of holiday in any year and she was not going to spend it with the Hamiltons. *They* had to heal. She was exhausted from work. Exhausted from financial worries, her husband's creations. She felt like that Dutch character in a fable, plugging fingers in the dyke. So, when Francesca learned about the Hamilton family gathering, instead of the holiday for which she had begged, she chose Boston. She chose Boston, alone.

"She's having an affair," was Laurence Hamilton's aside out of the corner of his mouth. Had Francesca chosen to go west, instead of Boston, her father-in-law's suspicion might have been justified. But in Boston, there was no one. The suggestion of an affair could not be farther from the truth. Fleeing, however, she was. And no sooner arrived, she was fleeing again, to something called Singing Beach.

She had only a book, towel and bathing suit in the knapsack, her wallet, and the clothes on her back. Her computer and suitcase, she had left back in Boston. The hotel where she stayed in Boston was close to a hospital, and was occupied mostly by nurses. One of the nurses told her about the beach when Francesca complained of the heat. The hotel was without air-conditioning. At night, afraid to go out alone, Francesca read books and tried to work, and tried to find air at the window, which she opened only a crack after dark, turning off the lights, to keep out the bugs. But the street noises and sirens made sleep impossible. She thought of her son. She had thought she would be able to sleep, now that her son, a "mouth breather," was not here to interrupt her with his cries for juice. She and her husband had a silent difference about that – but Francesca, who had suffered nightmares as a child, could not bear to keep him from their room, was secretly relieved each night when he trundled into their bed and found her face with his little hands in the dark. She could not sleep without him and knew that he would not be able to sleep without her. What would they both do for a week, without each other, without sleep? Surely, finally, exhaustion would overtake them?

Singing Beach got its name from the crabs. They would come out at night and bury themselves in the sand before dawn – their shells whistling, as they exhaled through the day.

All that afternoon, mothers and children bobbed in the ocean. Francesca, reading her book on the beach, eyed them above her glasses. She ate her chicken and rice salad, and sipped white wine, and took frequent dips in the ocean – brown and slender, unlike any other woman on this beach. She talked to no one, but she knew that this was not a tourist place. She was entirely strange – with her Mediterranean skin, her singleness – a woman without her child. This was where women whose husbands took care of them lived. They went daily to the sea with their children, and their husbands commuted to and from Boston. This beach belonged to women whose husbands were *working*, whose husbands were *taking care of their own*. These were plump American women – women who belonged. These were women who looked like turkeys made fat for the fall, for more children, discontented women, in an unmeaning way, who complained to each other of their lot, whose fat houses lined the coast, some within sight. When the beach began to clear, toward dinner, Francesca shivered in her skin, and wondered what to do with the night. She decided *not* to go back to Boston. Rather, she would head up the coast to the next stop or two.

And so Francesca arrived in Salem.

The bed and breakfast was a huge, sprawling, ancestral home. Francesca knocked on the door and a woman in her fifties answered. She looked at Francesca, in her durable Tilley khaki jump suit, with her knapsack, shivering on the porch, and invited her in. Francesca told her she was a journalist and had been delayed on the coast, needed a place to stay for the night, would be gone in the morning. "Here's your key. Here's the rule. No men allowed." The woman showed her a room, offered her a phone. Francesca phoned Boston, got them to remove her luggage to the concierge's desk. She didn't know when she'd be back. Then Francesca retraced her steps into town and stumbled upon a second-hand clothing store, where she could purchase clothing cheaply against the change in climate.

Francesca had never worn another's clothes. As she tried on a blue-jean outfit with leather fittings, the sales clerk told her that its original owner was a very wealthy woman about town, who never wore out her clothing but simply tired of it. So Francesca emerged from the store, the new-old clothes of a rich bored woman on her back.

There had been forty long-stem roses delivered to her office on her fortieth birthday. They had arrived in two boxes, without a note. After years of silence. She knew immediately who had sent them. She called the florist. The florist said their instructions were, on no account, to disclose the source. "Just answer me one thing," Francesca said. "Was the order made in Vancouver?"

Of course she had known. Wasn't this one of life's ironies? That her man of the west should be making a killing on Vancouver land speculation at the same time as her husband in Toronto was losing his shirt? In a fit of extravagance after his latest land flip, he had shared his celebration.

"This is a trick I learned from a Chinaman," he would later write. "The Chinaman sends letters to all the absentee landlords on the Gulf Islands, offering about a fifth of the assessed value. He operates a scam. My operation on Vancouver Island is above-board. At least I pay the price on the tax form. Prices were going up fast. This knowledge was my advantage over the absentee. Turned out the rate of rise was as much a surprise to me as to anyone. I ended up biting my nails while waiting for the term deposits to clear in six weeks. I had argued for the time and wished I hadn't, as the seller might have taken her chances with non-performance, the prices were climbing that fast. I could get triple. Wall Street, what? No? So anyway, there's my teeny little budget for the year. I tell you I don't use much… Why the roses? Because friends are rare? Because I wanted to think you might smile? Or is this just a chicken-shit explanation. Maybe I sent them because I love you."

In the cab from the Boston airport to her hotel, she had noticed the men with roses, arms outstretched. "What a wonderful gesture," she said to the cab driver, undeterred by the divider between front and back seats. "That a city should welcome its strangers with roses!" "You kidding, girl?" had said the incredulous cab driver. "Ain't nothing for free."

The proprietor of the bed and breakfast was watching television in the parlour, a room of dusty antiques. Francesca heard how this woman volunteered for the museum, was of Sicilian descent, had married an American husband, had left him when he turned abusive, had recently buried a mother, was happy as long as she made $2,000 a week playing penny stocks, bought on a Monday, sold on a Friday. Then she gave Francesca a private tour of the house, the various estate rooms and the corridors where the maidservants and men servants had travelled about. And here was Francesca's room. Francesca went to bed, leaving the light on. She slept in a canopy bed, with a chaise lounge against the far wall – something she thought of as a "day bed" or a "sick bed." She slept in her bra and underwear. She was cold to the bone, and covered herself with the blankets and a quilt. Dust filled her nostrils. With the weight of the quilt, she felt pinned to the bed.

Wrote her man of the west:

"I knew she was Italian right away. Not in one second, this was not a hurried pass in the city, but I knew, certainly. Mass of tangled dark hair, medium to slender boned, almond-shaped eyes that had a slight fold which made them sad and happy at the same time. Smooth skin of a colour – I don't know why some people call it olive, it's not green – I should say quite different from the pink with red over on Adam's English cheeks and brow. Her skin was darker. The lips were almost smoothly lined, not overly full, and bent upward at the corners of the mouth into a soft and genuine smile, sweetly –so unlike the television reporter's, typically a diesel-jawed baring of teeth. Then there are the little clues, the point with the nose (would a French lady do it that same way?), the swing of the wrist, those types of things. And did she remind me of you? Years later, I ask myself, whose image am I describing?"

Finally, mercifully, she fell asleep. She woke to the clap of two hands above her face. The night table light had been extinguished. She scrambled for the switch. There was nothing there, in the light. Was she delusional? She felt she was being mocked, was certain of a presence, a mischievous, taunting, non-malignant presence. She checked the two doors and the corridors off her room. The one was clearly the servants' corridor, in back of the house, where nothing breathed, and where she did not venture. The other was the shared corridor of owner and guests, with the bathroom on the second floor. Francesca struggled in the quasi darkness to the commode below, and relieved herself, sensing herself scrutinized. She made her way back to her room, and lay awake in the light of the electric lamp, until dawn, when she fell asleep and slept until noon.

Francesca declined the breakfast her patron offered, and the patron seemed relieved, riveted to her television screen watching the stocks. Francesca made inquiries about the coast. The bed and breakfast owner rallied herself sufficiently to dig out an old bicycle.

Francesca cycled down the coast. The bicycle wasn't a three-speed, or any speed. It was worse than anything she'd pedalled in her youth, or across campus during university, before she'd bought her first real mountain bike or hybrid. The chain was rusted, the seat too high. She was in pain after crossing a bridge, landing in some little town where, inexplicably, she bought a Battenburg lace harvest tablecloth. How would she get it back? Whatever was she thinking? It didn't even fit in the knapsack, but dangled from its double plastic bag off the handlebar, shifting her already off-centered balance.

"I had flowers all over the mantel and around the fireplace in the living room. I had a single white Battenburg lace tablecloth across two harvest tables in my dining room. The dappled effect of the setting sun in the back of the house was really lovely. And of course, everything is lovelier and mellowed over good wine. When I put together dinners like this I feel like an artist. The setting is as important to me as the food. I love to be surrounded by beautiful things. I have, after all, become an acquisitive woman, not taken over by it, but comforted by it. It is a real comfort to me at night to be reading a good book and to look around myself from my bed, enjoying the curtains, the paintings, the colours on the walls, the cleanliness and order of my environment. I love my house…"

She had told him about her things, saying nothing of their threatened loss, nothing of her husband, nothing of his insouciant risks.

And he had written back about his things and nothing of the women in his life:

"How did it get there? By much of my sweat in carrying piece by piece up a path from the dock, four years ago. Now it looks a permanent fixture. I share that disease with all men, who own in small amounts, small things: pride in the stuff seeps in. To think that eight years ago it was all in two suitcases. It seeps in even though you know about it beforehand, and feign to forestall its advance. Yesterday, I promised Al that I would not sell, now that the parklands have been finalized. He said they would stay as long as they were physically able to keep up things. At his age, who is he kidding? I could not believe him; I don't think he believed me…"

She parked her bicycle at a place that advertised lobster, and sat down to feed. Her table for two overlooked a yacht club on the Manchester coast. Her husband had always said the only way to eat lobster was to have it dripping off your elbows. The lobster was her afternoon project. When there was nothing left, the waiter removed her plate – looking at the demolishment of shells, sucked clean, and then at her.

On the way back to Salem, she ventured into a wealthy area of homes, set back far from the road and surrounded by gates. A security person came forward as she approached, squeaking and wobbly on her borrowed wheels – shifting the bag with the Battenburg lace from one handlebar to the other. She got off her bike, finally, and walked, no watering stands or grocery stores in sight. Was she out of her mind? All the while Francesca marvelled at the wealth. This had to be the fruit of generations of effort, a slow accretion, not something one person could attain through hard work alone, not in a single lifetime. This looked old, or illegal.

"Shacks. I plan about four of them. Studio, library, steam bath, with a gazebo. Large sheets of glass surrounded by wood, on wheels, that will form a glass wall, or roll back to the sides. Decks various places, and cedar catwalks connecting everything. There has to be a nominal house, in timber, concrete, steel, and glass. A guy, Formosa is his name, a fine art instructor with tenure at Langara College, built a bunch of shacks, the plan something like mine. We talked about our shack plans. I came to the conclusion that Formosa had never studied cell biology. A shack is more expensive than a house; costs range $5,000 to $10,000, even more, with appointments. The reason for the higher cost: there is a relation between the surface area expended and volume realized. Cell biologists are obsessed with the mathematics of this relation; calculations in the art that belongs to Galileo and others. Cost what they do, they are damned convenient. Small ones do not require a building permit, and therefore, can be erected in the no-build zones of the lot... I plan a steel structure, canvas covered, part open-air sculpting studio. I've done work in that form over the years.

"... I fabricate, in the tradition of my Finnish ancestors. There is this junkyard to which I go to purchase my materials. There are dogs, wilder than wolves. Normally, I am afraid of dogs, even little ones, but these I know. One bounds toward me, black and orange mottled, with straight hairs standing spiked, wolf-like. I get down, put out my hand; he smells it, knows it right away – the smell of welding smoke and burnt hairs; he loves the hand for its smell and licks it all over. Goes away after the moment, he knows I will be too busy for him. I shower and scrub down with sandalwood soap; the smell is still there after. No bar will erase it. I can sniff it now if I lean my chin on the knuckle of my thumb. The dogs know me: I am the man of the burnt-hair hands."

There had been no hiding the roses. Loyal woman that she was, she told her husband. She told him that there was this place on Pender Island, the man of the burnt-hair hands had called *her place*, "built for your eyes," and he described them as "shacks" but she knew better, from knowing the kind of man he was. They were sitting in bed, she and her husband, reading their respective books. "I can live with that," her husband had said. He gave her his crooked leer of a grin, one that came from having taunted a dog as a child. The dog had ripped off half his lip, necessitating the lip be sewn back onto his face – an invisible mend when his face was at rest, manifesting itself whenever he smiled: "I can live with that." He'd said it like a pimp. No jealousy at all. She wanted to smack him, the way she felt when she had opened his presents to her that Christmas and found "Work Horse Gloves," and he had laughed at her anger, at the present he had given his hardworking wife, that had insulted her to her core.

That spring she had put them on, anyway, just as she had put on the work horse boots, and gone out into her garden, and edged beds all around her property, and at 5:30 in the morning, a truck stopped, and this old Italian rolled down the window and said to her: "Now this I got to see. A woman with boots and a shovel. You got a husband?" And what had enraged her more than anything, more than being able to say yes, was that the husband was in bed, while she edged her own garden.

"Husband" is an ancient word, the meaning of which has been forgotten, a word transformed through various meanings and times, but meaning always essentially the same thing.

Housebonde, peasant owning his own house and land, a freeholder... One who tills and cultivates the soil; a cultivator, tiller, farmer, husbandman... The manager of a household or establishment; a housekeeper; a steward. Ship's husband: An agent appointed by the ship's owners to attend to the business of a ship while at port, esp. to attend to her stores, equipment and repairs, and to see that she is in all respects well found... And the verb: To husband: To till (the ground) to dress or tend (trees and plants), to manage as a Husbandman: To cultivate. She even found defined _a good husband: one who manages with thrift and prudence, who makes the most of; who saves and lays up a store of material things._

Francesca concluded: A husband is one who _takes care._ That is the word's essential meaning. A man who _takes care._ A husband is not a man who puts his woman and child at risk.

"They want only my personal guarantee," her husband had said to Francesca, when he first told her about the four houses to be torn down and reconstructed as million-dollar homes – the joint venture clients with whom he was also investing.

"Only your personal guarantee? Do you know what that's worth? That's your name, that's your reputation, that's me and our son, that's our home you've delivered up to this risk."

"Was it part of the point that you should yearn to see my retreat on Pender Island?" wrote her man of the west, contemporaneous with the service of legal process to her front door. Dogs. Her man of the burnt-hair hands had not begun to know dogs. Wilder than wolves were her husband's creditors. "Yes, it was part of the point. But you also have a safe haven of your own. It's in our life to see something, *again*. Neither you nor I are blind, but we each see our own way. Even in these letters we speak of common understandings: your house, my shacks."

The second night, she and the owner of the bed and breakfast went drinking in Salem. Francesca wore the new-old blue-jean and leather outfit, in which she felt like a rich bitch. Not herself. Dangerous and superficial. Capable of killing for a view. They were both hit upon by younger men. Men who had too much to drink. Men who were too young to know what they were doing. Silly men.

"How old are you?" Francesca asked one of them.

"You're too defensive about your age," he answered cockily.

"You didn't hear me. How old are *you*?"

"Twenty-eight."

"I'm forty-one. The beauty of turning forty is to know who you are, what you want, and how to get it. Right now, what I want is for you to go away."

The Sicilian bed and breakfast owner made a bark of a laugh. And as the whelp of a man skulked away from their table, Francesca laughed too. Was the brutal honesty borrowed too, like the new-old clothes on her back? Or was it something she had merely suppressed? She laughed and laughed. She laughed like she'd eaten her lobster earlier that afternoon, until nothing was left, not even her bones.

"Back in '78, I saw I could never offer you what you desired," he explained, when Francesca demanded an explanation – for why he had let her go, why he had not grabbed her by the hair and claimed his woman – why he had not protected her from the bad choices she was about to make, not rescued her from her life, how he had stood there at the train station and watched her leave, his strong fabricator's hands limp at his side. "My insight knows no bounds. I said I would not marry you (that was because I thought I loved you). And you laughed at me; silly girl, you really were much younger than I. Not now so different in age, now that (especially because) you have found an unabashed love for your son. Don't believe it about my insight? About you, I saw it faster than fast: right away. Should have said about you and me. I saw that I could not offer what you desired. I am honestly pleased to know you are happy, as you could not have been with me…"

He had been right, of course. She had believed it, at last. Had he claimed her, as she desired, they'd have ended in hate.

She and her husband were on a boat, at the island wedding of her husband's sister. The boat was for the adults, only – an after-ceremony cocktail party. She had been obliged to leave her son on shore, assured there would be supervision. All through the ride on the old *Seguin*, out onto Lake Joseph and back, she heard her husband above the engine, increasingly loud: how clever he'd been to time his suspension by the Law Society to coincide with the summer; and what a lucky man he was to have found such a hardworking wife, she who was managing the office for him during this suspension. A *woman well-found*. As if this were *his* accomplishment – having found her. She'd watched him, with his back to her, in the turn-of-century barbershop-quartet hat they'd given out to each man boarding the boat – that is any man who would take one – feeling her face burn with shame, thinking that a man with any pride or care for his own would never say such things – drunk or otherwise. And on the way back, she watched as her little son ran along the shore toward the point of the island, tripping now and again over his own feet or the exposed roots of the island pines, heading for the dock toward which the *Seguin* chuffed, agonizingly slow, having sighted his mother, and the clutch of his arms around her neck as she scooped him up, the peppery smell of his hair in her face, on her mouth, his dark curls threaded through her fingers. Oh, the clutch at her heart. *Mio figlio. Mio figlio.*

"Rain, drizzle, and more rain. I have been thinking about you, in the physical real sense, as opposed to someone with whom I ostensibly have a correspondence. So what physical? The strong grip of your hand, whenever our hands held, I looked over to see if there was someone larger, there, on the other end of that hand, not the little lady I could scoop with one arm. The scar you describe on your belly. I have had lovers like that. Your long black hair, not so long now, you tell me, the present colour – tinges, or added? I have felt passionate to savour the taste of you, to run my tongue from toenail to anklebone, and to lick even the last grey hair on your head. Your best, of course, is your smile, the honestly curving edges of a mouth putting upward the truth matched in expression by eyes and suggested by delight in posture of chin. An ageless reality there, only to be improved time for time in reaffirmation – variations on a theme. Smiling makes you beautiful."

"I've sometimes felt exquisite happiness in my garden. The gardening began again yesterday, in earnest. I raked leaves off the beds and saw the tender shoots of sprouting bulbs underneath. My husband, who bought me Work Horse Gloves as one of my presents last Christmas, was trying to encourage me this morning to chainsaw the old Chinese elms on one side of the house. I refused. I was up this morning at 5:30 making pizza (one half with sardines, black olives, Spanish onion; the other artichokes and ham). I can see my precious son from where I sit now (through the French doors off the master bedroom), climbing the cherry tree at the back of the property to terrifying heights. My husband is on the extension ladder tying rags to the branches of the willow and maple we're having trimmed this week by a professional arborist. Every now and then, when my nerves break down, I get up and holler through the door, 'Not so high, *be careful,*' – to absolutely no avail. My son has already taken to sighing resignedly, like his father, or ignoring me all together. He's the only one, you see. But I'm sure I'd be just as compulsive with two. When I explained to

my son why he had to come with me to the washroom, and why I could not leave him in the waiting
room with the optometrist's secretary, he asked me:
'Does she not know I'm precious?' Seriously. He
knows beyond his years. 'Will you die, Momma?' he
asked me the other day, his little mind already trou-
bled with cosmic questions. Life, right now, breaks
my heart. It has broken my heart since my son was
born. There are no midwives to coach us through.
*Am I doing all right? Is this normal? Is that how I will
sound, after transition, when the push-stage begins?* I
never howled. I have that to be proud of. And after
forty hours of quiet labour, they cut him out."

She was glad that she never told her man of the west
of her troubles. All the while she spoke of her son,
of her home, of her husband (how she had loved
saying those words, "my husband"), she never once
gave him any indication of her pain, painting such a
picture in rose. If he knew, he never let on. "I'm honestly pleased to know you are happy…"

Her man of the west was not the reason she left her
husband. The man of the "burnt-hair hands," her
fabricator who worked in iron, in the way of the

ancients. Who worked with his hands, and yet was of the "people of the head." He had stopped writing, inexplicably, a few years after he'd started again, in the fourth decade of her life. Cancer by sign, he had crawled back into the shell, burrowed into the sand. And the beach where he had lived had simply stopped singing. It had happened inexplicably – the same way the roses had arrived, on her fortieth birthday. By forty-four, she too had left. Deciding in the negative. Deciding not to go back. Not to remain, either. To pick up, at close of day, shake the sand out of her towel, and simply leave. She had not been disloyal, at least not in any traditional way. Just as she had not howled at the pains of labour; she had had the most unusual labour, her midwife had said – willing herself to sleep during transition. She would not howl at the pains of this delivery, either. She was proud of that. She had not needed another man in order to leave a husband. She'd done that all on her own. For all the right reasons. She had left *for herself. Herself alone*, like a crab, carrying her house, her shell on her back.

OPEN SESAME

"Sherma, make a chicken broth overnight that we may drink of it upon our return home."

"Ms. Malotti, are you all right?"

Only then did Francesca realize she was dream-speaking: Her Grenadian nanny's phone call had caught her in that deep stage of rapid eye movement, as if underwater, and too slow to surface to realize they were in Grenada, her boy lay sound asleep in the bed beside her, naked and pink from the afternoon's play at shuffleboard with the kindly elderly couple who had watched him while his Momma slept poolside, the Gravol from the plane ride having finally taken effect; that she was who she was, where she was, that there were no meal plans to be made, no trial returnable Tuesday, no husband, no worries; she was on holiday, courtesy of the very wealthy and influential client, Issa Nefrutta, whose island hotel would shelter them for the week and who had assured her *he would always be her friend.*

"Your result is a perfect example of brilliant lawyer skills and bad justice," Francesca's senior partner had announced, when she told him she had obtained a stay of the Nefrutta Canadian divorce proceeding. Now the client's wife would have to lit-igate him in that "nest of thieves," according to the senior partner – Trinidad and Tobago – where the bulk of his assets, influence, and substantial con-nections lay. When the satisfied client, Issa Nefrutta, offered his successful counsellor this vacation, she'd had her choice of Barbados, Trinidad, or Grenada.

Francesca had vacationed in Barbados with her husband on their last trip together, a holiday made miserable by the pinkeye contracted on the air-plane. Her eyes had sealed shut each night, they could be loosened only by the tea bags she used as salves – frightening the night security in the execu-tive lounge until he became used to her night-gowned presence, sleepless and despairing from a wordless anxiety she could not then name.

Her Grenadian nanny, Sherma, had placed a cup of tea in front of her the day her husband had moved out. Francesca had been sitting at her kitchen table, staring at the wall, her chin on her fists, when the cup of tea appeared wordlessly on the table before her.

"Hire me," Sherma had said to her during their job interview. "I promise you will never regret it." The only thing Francesca had known about Sherma was that her last employment had been to care for a dying woman. "You will never regret it." She was true to her word, taking care of Francesca's boy, and Francesca. An unexpected gift: a caregiver who took true care of the one who paid her.

So Grenada it would be: as much a gift of gratitude to Sherma as to Francesca. The influential client would have no idea about that, only that Francesca travelled with her boy and her nanny. Sherma would stay with her family, but would help her with the plane ride and the child, as Francesca's fear of flying went up in proportion to her level of commitment to life – ferocious since becoming a mother. The fear incapacitated her. The plan was for Francesca to ingest enough Gravol to sleep through the flight, while Sherma watched over Marco.

The Gravol, she took, but the events of that day had required too much attention.

There were the many suitcases with which Sherma had arrived at the airport, filled with Mr.

Noodle or other Canadian wonders for the extended Grenadian community back home. The extra weight cost Francesca an extra four hundred dollars – a burden she could ill afford at this early stage of her separation. But she could also not bear the look of disappointment on Sherma's face at the prospect of renting a locker for the burdensome luggage, the unspeakable disappointment of the intended recipients of Sherma's gifts.

And then there was the question at Grenadian Customs on arrival. "What is in the suitcases?" Innocent Canadian lawyer that she was, Francesca answered truthfully that she had no idea whatsoever what was in the suitcases, deferring to Sherma. Sherma inclined toward her and spoke quickly and quietly to her ear. "Say we are guests of Issa Nefrutta." So Francesca drew her diminutive presence up as regally and authoritatively as she could, and announced, "We are guests of Issa Nefrutta," and *open sesame,* the charm worked and the doors of Ali Baba's nest of thieves blew open, and there was Stroud, Issa Nefrutta's personal chauffeur and former Chief of Police of the island, waiting to receive Francesca, Francesca's son, and Francesca's Grenadian nanny – no questions asked. Francesca and her entourage and motley baggage loaded into the Rolls Royce of the tinted and bulletproof glass, without Francesca having to so much as lift a finger or speak another word.

Francesca looked at Sherma with a new appreciation of her wit or, at very least, intuition of the ways of the island from which she had departed and to which she now returned with her new employer, Francesca, and asked no questions of the *non sequitur*:

What is in the suitcases? We are guests of Issa Nefrutta.

"Bullshit baffles brains," a favourite saying of her now-former husband. Another: "You can fool some of them some of the time, most of them, all of the time."

This "We are guests of Issa Nefrutta" was the only time Francesca had ever resorted to ruse. Her only consolation was that, at the time, *it was the truth*.

What was in Sherma's baggage?

Her brother had dropped something off at the hotel where Francesca was staying as the guest of Issa Nefrutta. The brother had thought Sherma would be there, but she was with her Jehovah's Witnesses on that day. An insight, unrequested but delivered: Sherma had suffered heartbreak just before her departure for Canada. This was the reason for Canada. It was a very serious heartbreak. The man still lived in Grenada.

Francesca wondered: was there a child?

This didn't strike her as the Sherma she knew, but then, she didn't know Sherma, she didn't know about the heartbreak. She didn't know Sherma at all. But she knew that Sherma was no empty vessel, of the sort that makes the most noise, or hides robbers. Her secrets lay within, would not be heaved into her mouth. She was a good and honest servant, true to her word.

Issa Nefrutta was not amused to learn that his Canadian lawyer had taken a public bus to the public marketplace. Francesca and Marco had boarded the bus with Sherma, who had flagged it down for them from the public streets. They were the only whites on the bus, and on the bus her son inquired: "Mamma, are we rich?" "Hush, no, sweetie." "I just saw a car like our one…" There was no hushing him. He had no apprehension of harm. He was there with his Momma and Sherma, after all.

At the marketplace, with Sherma, they were safe. She bought them a coconut drink in a half shell of real coconut, and they milled about with Sherma's people, in Sherma's setting – safe, buying spices, beaded trinkets, a silk scarf at an Indian retailer, for home, being cared for by someone indigenous, of the island, who lived with them back in Canada.

The next day, Issa Nefrutta, who had heard of their escapades, insisted Francesca return again, with Stroud, on a tour of a different sort. Did Issa contemplate that his former Chief of Police would take them to his former headquarters and show them the spot where the insurgents had been gunned down – bullet holes in the wall? Bullet holes in a supposedly bloodless revolution? Stroud counselled Francesca not to ask political questions, nor to seek answers of her own. But what kind of message was this to deliver to a lawyer: what to make of Stroud's advocacy against asking questions, against seeking answers?

And then, in the public market place, seated with her son in the backseat of the bulletproof vehicle with the winged decoration on the front hood, Francesca watched in helpless horror through the tinted glass as the Rastafarian approached, raised his arms in combat-like position, and clicked the imaginary gun of his hand, balanced in the crook of his arm, his open eye cocked on the target of her son. There is such a thing as the wrong place at the wrong time. In Issa Nefrutta's bulletproof Rolls Royce, they were such things. They were marks. Francesca knew Issa had moved his own children off the island for their safety. The legal arguments Francesca had used to persuade the Canadian Court of their "substantial connection" to Grenada, notwithstanding the move to safer ground, now came back to haunt her. Francesca and Marco were caught on the screen, and the illusionist, with his fingers in front of the lighted projection machine – fluttered dove into gun.

On the island is a church with a bell. Stroud took them there. Beside the church is a graveyard. Stroud told them how, during the revolution, it was reported that persons had jumped from these cliffs. The bell has a rope. The rope dangled, irresistibly. And in the end, Francesca had not been able to resist. Her young son was appalled when his mother did this. The bell rang for funerals and for weddings. Stroud told them this. But on this day, Francesca rang it, for herself and her son. For the fact they were there, alive, and *it, the bell,* was there.

For the *I don't know why*. Just to hear it ring. What it might sound like. For the *joy of it*. For the anarchic *hell of it*.

By the time they got back to the hotel, the whole island had heard. Issa Nefrutta had heard. Issa Nefrutta's lawyer had rung the bell. How to govern this Canadian lawyer of his – who had no sense of decorum?

Do not let your son pat the dogs on the beach. They are wild dogs, and are full of disease.

Francesca watched, as the bitch was mounted, one after another, by the pack. Francesca studied the expression on the bitch's face. What was it? Passive? Barely interested? Accepting, almost, of the exchange. But what did the bitch get out of it? Protection, possibly? Food offerings? It was not obvious. "What are they doing, Momma?" "Pay no mind, they are just playing. That's what dogs do, they play."

Do not treat your servant too well. Servants respect authority, not kindness.

The next day they were going to walk the beach together. Sherma did not possess a bathing suit. Francesca gave her a black bathing suit, one of the four she had packed. This was the one from Florence, with the black scalloped collar, the fringe of green sparkling thread, tied behind, at the neck. And she lent her the Florentine scarf, of multi colours, to be worn like a sarong. It would blow in the ocean wind like a small glistening sail. The finishing piece – her white hat, with the black lace fringe, Francesca's fanny hat, worn with the right side turned up saucily, and the bow behind, a magnificent, seductive hat, one that bespoke success and even wealth. With these decorations and her large dark glasses, Sherma looked like a black Jacqueline Kennedy Onassis. She looked gorgeous, in the way of a vindicated young woman who can wear anything. Francesca would never again wear that bathing suit or that scarf or hat, because these belonged to Sherma now and would be forever part of this day – Sherma's day, this was her day, and Francesca walked behind her, ten paces behind, collecting sea shells, as Sherma walked, her long black legs making modest tracks in the sand, with Francesca's pink son at her side, and Francesca watching the sensation her servant created – the returning woman, could hear the word on the island, the word in town, the word that was out – that Sherma had returned, that Sherma had returned *in style*. The best vengeance, absolutely, is to live well. That day Sherma vibrated – an instrument, in tune with her world.

And what was Francesca's part of this day? That she could aid and abet another woman.

"Ms. Malotti, you will never know what this has meant to me. I am so very grateful…"

Francesca knew. No thanks were required. This was vindication by extension.

Do not treat your servant too well…

Do not walk the beach alone at night. If you wish privacy, my security guards will follow you, at a distance, from the shore.

The Ferryman

> *"Ferry me across the water,*
> *Do, boat-man, do."*
> *"If you've a penny in your purse,*
> *I'll ferry you."*

"I have a penny in my purse,
   And my eyes are blue;
   So ferry me across the water,
   Do, boat-man, do."

"Step into my ferry boat,
   Be they black or blue,
   And for the penny in your purse
   I'll ferry you."

Francesca's son had to memorize this song so he could sing it as one of the Toronto Children's Chorus by their return to Canada. Alone on the beach, of a morning, unaware of Issa's security guards or of Issa's eyes, Francesca sat cross-legged on the pink sand, facing the ocean, her son safely tucked in the crib of her crossed legs, the *Introductory Songbook* of the Grade 1 level of the Royal Conservatory of Music open in front of them, singing with a passion for the boatman and the woman whose colour of eyes to the boatman was completely immaterial, who was doing it, if at all, for the penny in the purse, thinking about the ones who carry us across the water, who are rarely the ones who meet us on the other side, wondering what these words of Christina G. Rossetti were doing in a Vocal Repertoire Album intended, supposedly, for children? And what of that non sequitur: "I have a penny in my purse and my eyes are blue." What currency is blue eyes? And whose boat had Francesca stepped into? What act of faith did this take, black or blue, whether penny in her purse, or otherwise – she, a woman, so far from home? A woman, alone. A woman with child. Alone.

I will always be your friend.

She was supposed to meet him for cocktails. She assumed at the hotel bar, beside the pool, where she could be mindful of her son, unlike the day of their arrival.

What had the elderly couple that had cared for her little boy thought of this mother, while she, unconscious with the delayed affects of the Gravol, had slept? There is a picture of Francesca asleep on a lounge chair, curled fetal, with a book of short stories by Alice Munro gripped in her right hand, pressed beneath her cheek, her face closed with sleep, but for the open mouth. Seeing this picture developed, which her son must have taken, Francesca imagines the sound of snores, possibly drool.

Around the hat with the black lace fringe is a halo of fuschsia hibiscus her son carefully picked and arranged, in preparation for this picture of his Momma.

Now the son protects his mother. There will be no cocktails with Issa and Francesca. It has turned cold. At 6:30 p.m., the sun setting, the wind is up from the ocean. Francesca assumes Issa has stood her up, while Issa, from his perch in the executive suite, had assumed likewise. Francesca is delivered, is relieved. She takes her boy to their room and gives him a hot bath. She follows his hot bath, with her own, and they both retire early.

Francesca sends Issa Nefrutta a final bill, upon her return to Canada, which reflects her sense of the true value of the result she has achieved on his behalf. She sends the bill along with her gracious thanks for his gift of this holiday – the first she has taken in years. Francesca has weighed most care-fully the issue of her bill. What recourse does she have if he refuses to pay? She senses what he has intended by this trip. It becomes very difficult to bill, having received this holiday as his gift. But ultimately, not difficult at all. The bill reflects what her services are worth, what she herself is worth. She hasn't asked for the gift. Nor has she abused his hospitality, nor deceived him in any way. She simply does not deliver his latest expectation, which is outside their retainer, in any event. What harm in that? She has remained his true and loyal servant, will not compromise the solicitor and client relationship. For the penny in your purse, not for anything else, has she carried him across the water. So, Francesca holds her peace during the silence that has followed on her bill. As the morning begins to dawn on a month following her return, Shahrzad suspends her story to the next time and extends her own life thereby, just as surely as Francesca rang a church bell, once upon a time, in Grenada.

ZACHARY
AND THE SHAMAN

Let me have speech with you.
– Come, my dear love, –
The purchase made, the fruits are to ensue,
That profit's yet to come 'twixt me and you.
　　　　　　　　　　　—Shakespeare, *Othello*

Zachary left home at the age of fifteen, backhanded off the dinner table by an abusive father, with only fifty-six cents in his pocket. He hitchhiked north of Great Slave Lake, where he convinced a commercial trawler fisherman he was older than he looked. That first summer of fishing, he earned $22,000. Not bad, for a fifteen-year-old kid! And he drove cab and ambulance that winter before he went on the dole, or so Zachary told Francesca. After four years of not seeing or contacting a single family member, he chanced upon his brother in butt-hole nowhere. The brother had just killed his first patient on an operating table, had grown a beard, and was thinking of dropping out of medical school. The two Hamilton brothers, both having grown beards, went on a bender together. All her then-future husband could remember of their bender was being cut by a beer bottle across the palm of his hand in a barroom brawl, such that he lost sensation in two fingers. He would often demonstrate his imperviousness to pain by holding a match under his palm. The other result of the bender was that Zachary convinced his older brother to return to medical school; his older brother convinced Zachary to enter law school. In further circuitous consequences, Francesca's then-future husband would land in Toronto, where he met Francesca at the bar admission course.

"I fell in love with his stories, like Desdemona to Othello."

"Ah," her senior partner remarked, while waiting for the Law Society discipline hearings that would lead to her husband's suspension (not yet his disbarment, which wouldn't come for another fifteen years), "I *get it*, now – the attraction, but not how someone as bright as you could fall for a story."

Did Francesca *get it*? This seduction through the tales Zachary could tell? Certainly, he had a great many of them. Her favourite was about the Shaman...

THE SHAMAN

Zachary's woman at the time was named Moshe. Her father was a Shaman. Years later Moshe would stab the drunken Shaman to death while he was attempting to rape her. By then she would be married to a German. The German engineer paid for her legal defence, and she got off lightly. But when Zachary had met Moshe, they were both fifteen. He remembered fondly the brief summers, and berry picking, and being permitted to sleep while Moshe's people picked berries around him, his dozing interrupted only by the buzzing of insects. And so Zachary learned something of another culture. And indulgence. Or lack of acquisitiveness. He spoke highly of the absence of possessiveness among the Inuit. Children belonged to the community, and not so much to their birth parents. If you needed a kayak to cross an inlet and there was one on shore, you used it. There were no allegations of theft, no hard feelings. If you arrived somewhere and the cabin was empty but you found a store of frozen meat, no one thought anything of helping himself.

Zachary and Moshe spent one winter holed up in a cabin. Zachary read and took long walks every couple of days for a chocolate treat called "cherry blossoms" which Moshe adored.

Although Zachary insisted that he'd had no contact with his family during this time, he must have made contact with his mother. This is the only explanation for the letter Francesca finds many years later, in the basement file cabinet:

…I would like to thank you for your monetary support. I could get along out at the lake, but living here is so much better. It is unbelievable, actually. Both Mr. and Mrs. Huber are young and active, so it is a good atmosphere. I am glad to have school in my future again…

So, the story of the Shaman…

Zachary had gone with a group of the Inuit men in search of the seal. The men built an igloo for the night and then retired inside. The Shaman drilled a hole through the ice to the ocean, to conjure the spirit of the seal. The igloo filled with mist. Zachary sat blind in the mist, listening to the incantations and stories of past hunts. Then suddenly, there was a thud and a whooshing sound. The mist that had permeated the igloo, that had blinded him during the storytelling, evaporated. The Shaman was nowhere to be seen. He was gone, and with him, the mist. When Zachary recovered from his surprise, he saw a hole blown through the side of the igloo. The next day, the men hunted a great many seals.

That was the whole of it, this story, but Zachary had a way of drawing it out – the churning of the pole through the thick ice to the ocean surface; the suffusing of mist into the igloo, and he would take so long in the recounting of this that Francesca would grow impatient for him to get to the point, and particularly this day, knowing her senior partner had patience for no man, least of all her errant husband. They must keep the senior partner entertained, or he would be off to remunerative tasks, not this, surely, not this taking care of his junior lawyer with the husband-of-many-transgressions. Of all men, apart from her father, her senior partner was the only man to have ever taken care of her. She felt grateful.

"I know Francesca. She is an honest woman. If you ever, *ever* do this to her again you will answer to me, personally."

The "this" was Zachary having involved her, compromised her reputation for honesty, her fidelity to the truth.

"I hear the music. *'Good idea at a bad time. I did it for my family.'* No, my friend, you have a serious problem." And to Francesca he said privately: "This man will always be trouble for you, as long as you are with him. There will be no escape, unfortunately, now that you're connected through the child."

Sins of the father: She hadn't got that fully yet either.

Zachary's paternal grandfather had been a plantation owner in New Guinea. So Zachary's father, Laurence Hamilton, had the distinction of being the first white man to hike to the top of the highest mountain in New Guinea, when he was only fifteen, guided by indigenous workers who really knew the route. But in New York, with the annual meeting of the World Explorer's Club, it was the white man who had taken the accolades.

Laurence Hamilton, a bomber pilot during World War II, had learned to fly in Port Colborne, Ontario, where Zachary's maternal grandfather, Horatio Kroll, was the owner and founder of Beaver

Boots, employer to half the town. Laurence Hamilton there met and wooed the factory-owner's daughter Elizabeth. After the war, with the New Guinea estate confiscated for unpaid taxes, the dashing fighter pilot knew how to butter his own bread. He had returned to Port Colborne bearing a bag of pearls from the former New Guinea estate. Ever resourceful, these Hamiltons were aided by their swashbuckler looks, and where the looks failed, by charm, by The Story, the Tall Tale, the Excellent Exploit. "Bullshit baffles brains" was another of Zachary's favourite sayings. "You can fool some of them some of the time, most of them all of the time."

Where is Francesca going with these thoughts? She is trying to explain to herself how a bright woman could become enamoured of a Zachary-of-the-Shaman story.

"I don't want to hear my sweet boy's name dragged in the mud," Francesca's mother-in-law had said to her when Francesca had tried to explain to her (a woman she did genuinely respect), why she was leaving Zachary. So Francesca never got the chance to tell her. Silence. True to her Calabrian heritage. Silence was as it should be. Zachary was a mother's son. Where would she be, in the defence of her own?

Running down a hospital corridor, demanding to know who was the last person in her room — this, within an hour of her caesarean surgery, believing that the last person must have stolen her baby. Stood at the nurse's station, militant, a lioness in the defence of her cub, then briefly confused. The nurse took hold of her hand, kindly. "We have to check in on you." With the nurse's gentle touch, Francesca realized she was delusional.

Zachary's father had been an only child. He had a pet pig in New Guinea. This was before the parents decided to send him away to boarding school. Zachary's New Guinea grandfather divorced his wife while his son was away at boarding school. The young Master Hamilton, then only six, never saw his mother again. How odd that a man who had been an only child, separated from his mother at such an early age, would go on to sire six children.

Many years after their separation, Francesca decides to clean out an old file cabinet. She discovers that Zachary used the second drawer for some personal papers. Like an explorer, she takes a quick reading of the compass, settles down to discover the man with whom she spent a decade of her life.

ZACHARY'S LETTERS TO HIS MOTHER

Dear Mom,

In the package you sent me, I had a tooth brush. Im swimming.

I cut my finger. I didn't cry. We are picked up for camp. We are having a Indian night,

Your son,

Zachary

Francesca knows when this letter was written. Zachary's mother's sixth and youngest child, a Down syndrome girl, had died after years of illness. Zachary's mother suffered a nervous breakdown. Zachary's father sent Zachary's mother on a world tour, arranging for her to stay in the homes of his veteran, fighter-pilot buddies. She was gone for a year. Zachary was only six at the time – too young to be separated from his mother.

"My sweet boy. I won't have you bad-mouthing my sweet boy…"

Dear Mom,

It was a real treat to see you and the family. It is said that one really never knows what they have until it is gone.

By now you have seen a copy of my marks. Everything can be pulled up a little more, with a big leap expected in English…

BABE'S FILE

In a file marked "Babe's File" Francesca finds her own letter to Zachary, written on hotel paper from St. Andrews-by-the-Sea, New Brunswick. It was their first holiday together after marriage. Zachary had to return to Toronto to try to find a job, having learned of his termination as an associate lawyer on a check-in call to his employer during their first week away. Zachary had promised Francesca he'd have a job by the time she returned. He would paint their front porch, he promised.

My sweet Zachary—

I have tried to reach you many times by phone. My gallivanter.

I have just finished dinner – scallops and spaghetti done the way I did it in St. John for you. No matter how many years I have lived as a single woman, eating alone is never something to which I have accommodated. Life is diminished when there are things we cannot share.

I wish I had returned with you. I miss the soft feel of your beard, the devil in your brown eyes. How I miss your always smiling, cheerful face. Where do you find your hopefulness?

Love, Francesca

WELLAND COUNTY PUBLIC SCHOOL,
GRADE 4 PROGRESS REPORT:
A BOY WHO PERSISTS IN EVADING THE RULES

A well-mannered boy. Although intelligent, Zachary will do no more than is absolutely necessary.

Letters from the Headmaster, St. Andrew's College, Aurora, Ontario

Dear Mr. Hamilton,

Zachary's attitude deteriorated soon after Xmas. He is guilty of rash, impulsive acts, giving little prior thought to the consequences.

Dear Mr. Hamilton:

I regret to have to inform you that Zachary has been reported to the office for smoking. He knows the rules: A second instance will involve a gating. A third offence will bring automatic expulsion. More fundamental is the loss of confidence that is inevitably produced in a boy who persists in evading school rules.

Rash, Impulsive Acts, With Little Thought to the Consequences

We have choices, surely. Yes, we are born with a set of givens, and become ever more who we essentially are: that has always been Francesca's belief. But Zachary had a choice who to emulate as his hero. He had many possibilities.

Mrs. H.H. Kroll (Irene) passed away in the Port Colborne General Hospital on Monday, September 2nd, 1968. Irene Kroll was the wife of Horatio Kroll, founder of Beaver Boots and upstanding member of this community, whose annual picnics and acts of charity need no mention.

Irene Kroll had been active in civic life for many years, being a true first lady of Port Colborne always at her husband's side for public ceremonies. She was a regal hostess and an active member of St. James Anglican Church. She was one of the stalwart workers of the St. James Ladies Guild, and one whom, despite the last years of ill health, always wore a smile.

For many years we have been awed and impressed by the civic record of Horatio Kroll and all he had given to this city. But very seldom has anyone paid tribute to the gracious woman who stood at his side. In her quiet way she reigned over civic functions and was a gracious and charming hostess. She seldom, if ever, refused to pour at the endless rows of tea tables.

She is survived by her husband Horatio and two daughters, Mrs. Laurence (Elizabeth) Hamilton of Ottawa...

Zachary's father, Laurence, the former fighter pilot, needed a job. Horatio Kroll had a boot factory. He set his son-in-law up as foreman, elevated him to plant manager. Then Zachary's father started his own boot factory, in competition with his father-in-law. Talk about biting the hand that feeds you! The men continued in unhappy rivalry. Unable to tolerate the unkempt nature of his daughter Elizabeth's front lawn, Horatio Kroll used to fire up the lawnmower at 6:30 of a Saturday morning, right under his daughter's bedroom window. Laurence Hamilton retaliated by picking up the family and moving to Ottawa. That must have killed Horatio Kroll – the loss of his daughter and grandchildren.

Years later, when Francesca visits Port Colborne with Zachary and their son, one of the neighbours comes out of her house to greet them on the street.

"My God, I thought I was having a vision. This dear little boy is the spitting image of Zachary. I thought it was Zachary, born again, running down this street!"

Zachary knocks on the door that used to belong to his grandparents. He asks the new owners if he can show the place to his wife. True to small-town hospitality, the owners let them come in. Zachary regales them all with stories: How he used to stop in at this very kitchen door on the way home from school; how his grandmother had this cookie jar, just inside the door, on this very counter. His grandmother, Irene Kroll, would holler out when she heard the lid clang and the bang of the screen door. How Zachary makes Francesca laugh with the stories of Irene and Horatio (Rache) Kroll, how Irene would pump up her lungs – those enormous, stalwart, Anglican breasts – holler down to the shed near Lake Erie where Horatio would be hiding, how he'd pretended never to hear her, though the whole neighbourhood could. "Rache, Rache…" Didn't matter, then, that he might be the founder of Beaver Boots. Francesca laughs until the tears roll down her cheeks, as Zachary portrays Irene's pumping breasts, the dragon fire of her fury, when Rache ignores her.

Rache died at the age of 94. He'd ignited himself on a stove where he was cooking, down near the lake, and threw himself into the icy water of Lake Erie to extinguish the flames. The fire didn't kill him but the shock of the cold lake rendered him feeble, and Horatio Kroll died a few years after that.

Francesca loves Grandpa Kroll, though she'd never met him. She loves the tough face she met in a photograph, with its map of wrinkles, the wry smile, the sharp, witty eyes that twinkle with that direct, honest stare he plants straight at the camera. Francesca knows from Zachary that he stayed with his Grandpa in his thirteenth year – the year his father took the family to Ottawa. Zachary refused to go. It was in Zachary's fifteenth year that his father backhanded him off the dinner table and Zachary hitchhiked north of Great Slave Lake.

There were two ways Zachary could have gone. He could have been like the man who would set up in business competitively against the father-in-law. Or Zachary could have become like the founder of Beaver Boots. Which would he choose?

"Promise me only one thing," Francesca asks, when she accepts Zachary's hand in marriage. "Promise you will make me proud of *my choice*."

Zachary promised.

"He seems to like me," she explained to her senior partner, announcing the marriage.

"Hello? What's not to like?"

Law Society of Upper Canada Ontario
Discipline Committee: Re. Hamilton

The Solicitor was part of a group of five investors, acting as the lawyer for the joint venture. Shortly before the investment required refinancing, the Solicitor transferred his interest in his principal asset to his wife. He did not disclose his changed financial position to the other investors, one of whom advanced additional funds personally for the refinancing...

...

In an Addendum to their Marriage Contract dated March 26, 1990, the Solicitor and his wife described the consideration for the transfer as being their unequal contributions to the matrimonial home and continuation of the marriage, which, at that time, was in jeopardy.

CONVOCATION HEREBY ORDERS that Zachary Hamilton be suspended for a period of two (2) months, such suspension to commence the 1st day of July...

Background music

"They only want my personal guarantee."

"*Only?* Do you know what that's worth? That's your name. Your reputation. You lose that, you lose everything…"

The consideration for the transfer was the continuation of the marriage, which at the time was in jeopardy…

More music

"I'm not going to audit our joint account. I'm going to take you at your word. You tell me how much you *stole* from me and our son. Then you're going to sign this house over to me, and that dollar amount, however much you say you stole, and all the future unequal contributions, and me remaining in this marriage, is the consideration. As long as I own the house, it's safe for our son. You keep your interest, it's lost to your creditors, the whole thing, including me. Take your pick. Trust them. Or trust me."

Running down a hospital corridor, in the logic of delirium, within an hour of surgical birth, demanding to know… Stands there, half naked, militant, a lioness in defence of her cub. They take her hand, gently, take her back to her bed. Running down a hospital corridor in bare feet, trembling from shock newly severed from her baby. Determined to find him – her one, only child.

She would have run through fire. She would have lied, stolen, laid waste to generations of integrity. She'd have done anything for this child.

For she had looked into his face, with those wide-open eyes, searching for her, blindly, she, who had heard his first cry, who could not stop crying, had heard that tall ships, passing before the mouths of caves at the very moment sun entered, as through a shutter, left a negative of the ship on the back of the cave; imprinted with him, his face like a negative upon her mental plate. She'd have done anything for this child. This child of one hour. This innocent child. Blood of the father fresh in his veins.

"He's having an affair, and you should too."

They are standing at the cash register, in the men's section of the Hudson's Bay Company, on their way to oral questioning. Her senior partner has bought himself dress slacks and suggests she buy a pair for her husband, as they're on special. "What are you, too cheap? I don't pay you enough?" She confesses to not knowing her husband's pant size. "He's lost weight," she explains.

"He's having an affair. A man only loses weight when he's prowling."

The young man at the cash turns beet crimson. As embarrassed as he, Francesca laughs and tries to make light of it.

"Let me introduce my boss – the one inciting his loyal servant to marital infidelity."

Her senior partner was away at the time of her husband's eventual disbarment. Learning of the Law Society's decision, fifteen years after the discipline hearing at which he had represented Francesca's husband, the only comment of her senior partner was: "Poor kid, with this father."

TRIBUNAL DECISIONS, 2007

Zachary Hamilton (1985), was found to have engaged in professional misconduct for participating in or knowingly assisting in dishonest or fraudulent conduct to obtain mortgage funds under false pre-

tences in connection with purchase, sale and mortgage transactions on six properties…

By Decision and Order, the Hearing Panel orders
that: The license of the licensee shall be irrevocably
revoked…

"I never would have had the courage for this."

Francesca is looking at the photograph of her son
and former husband, their arms both crossed cockily in identical poses, in wet suits and goggles, flip-
pers, standing on the ocean floor, dozens of reef
sharks circling about. It is not the scuba diving
with sharks – although she fails to comprehend
the risks her former husband continues to take
with their one, only son – but the scuba diving, itself.

"I'm too claustrophobic to breath through a
tube."

"It's the fastest way of entering new worlds,"
Zachary tells her.

"Only because our son is here, only because I
know about the sharks, after the fact, do I forgive
you."

She looks at him coyly. They begin to laugh – he with that crooked grin of his; Francesca at first shyly, and then hysterically. They laugh and laugh. Husband and wife. Not in years has she laughed like this. Not since that early morning, when Francesca had tried to pen a reason to the Law Society brief, the two of them drinking scotch, trying to explain – why he had done it, why she had title to the house transferred – trying it out this way, then that, until she throws pen to air. "Why? *To defeat, hinder, delay and defraud your creditors.*" Laughing into the dawn – shameless co-conspirators that they are, partners in crime. Choking on the words. Choking on the scotch. Choking…

"He didn't write this, did he? I thought not. Your husband is incapable of *your brilliant advocacy.*" Her senior partner's praise for the craft that garnered a husband *only* a two-month suspension. It wasn't until fifteen years later that the irrevocable revocation would come to pass.

"I never would have had the courage for this."

"Only because our son is here, do I forgive you."

And for just a moment, staring at the photographs of this underworld of the Bahamas, to which he and her son have escaped, impervious to the sharks, does Francesca remember the almost irresistible charm. It is the charm of crooks, scallywags and daredevils. But for the father... Only for this split second is she slightly persuaded that, yes, *he* had been worth the risk.

What will this child turn out to be?

"I got a 90, Ma," her son says to her, a sheepish smile on his face. He does not really expect her to commend him over his achievement of his Ontario Hunting Licence. Francesca doesn't have to say a word, just to stare at the book he leaves on the coffee table in their living room. *Chronic wasting disease... black bear... stray bullets...* In all the years of separation she has never been able to accommodate this, to overcome her fears. *How many times has she seen the body of her boy draped in her arms?*

But stop. Do not even go there. For Francesca knows the power of conjurers and poets – a power so overwhelming it can drive Othello to murder his Desdemona, seals surface at a Shaman's incantations, put real to the face of mere possibilities. *Running down a hallway…*

Yet this will be: this child will grow up, her own good, sweet boy, to make this mother proud – will go away to university, will become a man to make his own journey to destinations as yet unknown, but assuredly far, far away – perhaps as far away as New Guinea, or north of the Great Slave, or to Antarctica and ocean floors – for this wanderlust flows in his veins as assuredly as Francesca's love for the stories he will deliver, whenever it is he returns home.

CHÂTEAU STORIES

Whatever propels her to *Château Cuisine* is as mysterious as where and how she came by the book – although she could follow the sequence, logically enough. The pheasants were a gift from a man who ate nothing he himself did not kill or forage, like the *chanterelles* that would accompany them. The preparation of the pheasants will occur New Year's Day, in honour of the new life she is determined to create – hence the need for a new and challenging recipe. And who better to do game than the French? So Francesca, casting about in her recipe books, comes up with the promising title of *Château Cuisine – et voilà! Faisan à la Massena* (roast pheasant stuffed with *chanterelles* and oyster mushrooms); *faisans en escabèche* (oil and vinegar braised pheasants in aspic); and *faisans à la Chartreuse* – the three possibilities the text offers, in sumptuous tribute to a heritage of castle architecture and rich taste.

In celebration, Francesca pours herself another large glass of the Crystal Head Vodka a grateful client has given her this Christmas, and looks at the university-aged man-child sprawled on her couch, home for the holidays, asleep with the excesses of exams, Christmas and alcohol. Her one, only son. They were supposed to put up the last of the Christmas tree decorations together: photos of her son's Christmases past, twenty-two in total, including the one where Francesca is pregnant with him, standing in front of their first Christmas tree. But her son crashed on the couch immediately after dinner.

So Francesca put up these decorations alone. Some of the photographs included his father. She didn't think it fair to exclude these. She plugged in the lights and stood back to survey her creation. Laden with the weight of years, this year's Christmas tree is spectacular.

Feeling suddenly cold, although in front of the fireplace, she draws the Christmas throw more tightly about herself, and tucks back into her book of *Château Cuisine,* to learn about "trussing a bird" with needle and string in the glossary of explanations, already mentally removing the powdered gelatine from the recipe for *faisan en escabèche,* and replacing it with the four small firm apples, peeled, cored, thickly sliced into rings and halved, to be flamed

with 4 tablespoons of Armagnac from the recipe
for *faisan à la Massena*. She thinks of adding the
wild mushrooms to the already-prepared stuffing
in her freezer, of fresh walnuts, seasoned bread-
crumbs, carrots, and finely sliced fennel (to add her
own personal, Sicilian touch) to her New Year's creation – wondering about *what is upsetting her, what
dark presence squats at the corner of her mind, a gar-
goyle on the buttresses of her imagination*, when she
turns the pages to the source of the book—

    Good memories... the start of many more
    David & Olga
    Christmas, 1992

And there it is – the Château du Marais, where she
and her then toddler son and her husband stayed for
two weeks with David and Olga, new acquaintanc-
es from her son's "stay-and-play." Her husband
Zachary had suggested she invite them on this holiday – with his Scot's frugality (only generous when
someone else was footing the bill) – not wishing to
waste anything, when future profit might be in the
balance, not least of all the five rooms with en-suite
bathrooms in their wing of the Château du Marais,
invited them on impulse (his recipe for living), as
they barely knew David and Olga, and their child

Alessandra. Francesca herself had sublet the wing from her senior partner, with another partner to follow, upon their departure. The real generosity belonged to her senior partner, who had suggested it in the first place – using two weeks of his four, as he had tired of the Château du Marais as he tired of most everything, including his over-zealous junior.

"You take the law too seriously. You need to lighten up, have some fun. Go to France, with *that husband of yours*. Take a few friends."

How to explain that she was working too hard as his junior to have any friends. David and she had met early Saturday mornings, watching their respective children (her Marco, David's Alessandra) play alongside each other in the church basement, while their respective spouses slept late. They quickly discovered something in common, apart from having children the same age: they were both "morning people" – their personal hearts-of-darkness tending to come in the early afternoons. Francesca liked the fact that David shaved and was the only father not in jogging pants. He actually came to these Saturday mornings respectably dressed.

And there it is, too – the artificial lake, over 500 metres long, where Francesca had rowed the little boat for her son, and where a small plane had flown over and landed, Francesca frantically pointing their little craft to meet the swell – the artificial lake, normally so still, reflecting all it sees, such that it is known as "the mirror," says the text, and the grounds of which, rich in escargot, have been strolled by the likes of Chateaubriand and Madame de Staël.

Under the American duchess, the Château du Marais again became an exclusive haven for Europe's nobility: her granddaughter, known as the Duchesse de Sagan, is the present owner. She shares with her three children the task of maintaining the Château and its outbuildings, which include an orangery, a museum devoted to family history and a functioning water mill, besides twenty-five hectares of parkland. "It is so hard to preserve," laments Comtesse Guy de Bagneux, the Duchesse's daughter. "We are only 40 kilometres from Paris. Highways and power lines encroach all the time." For Comtesse Guy the menace seems all the more threatening – her most nostalgic childhood memories are of intimate afternoon tea in the park with her legendary American grandmother. "The chef prepared special cakes, but what we all loved best was cinnamon toast."

And in the kitchen that is part of their "wing," Francesca prepares *tortellini in brodo*, using fresh thyme, rosemary and parsley from the Château's gardens, for her one, only son, and Olga and David, and her husband, of course. She and Zachary shop at the local marketplaces every morning, and he convinces her to try unique foods, including horse. She makes *cheval à la cacciatore* from a recipe she carries in her head, along with a rabbit (*fricassée de lapin aux trois racines*), rabbit stew with root vegetables for the less adventurous. Together, the two couples drink copiously of wine, while Olga's and David's child eats only wieners and coloured Cheerios. And at the open window during mealtimes, David sits guard, with his long legs, making sure that neither child falls to his or her death on the terraces below.

She discovers something in common with Olga. One day as Francesca is deboning the boiled chicken, Olga asks, "What are you going to do with that?" She speaks of the gristle at the tail of the breastbone.

"Oh, I always eat it, my little secret in the kitchen. It's my favourite part of the chicken – my peasant roots!"

"Then I have them, too, because it's *my* favourite part of the chicken."

With the next chicken she prepares, Francesca serves up the gristle to Olga, on the chipped Limoges discovered amid the saucers of their kitchen cupboard. Olga laughs as she removes the paper napkin to discover this gift, Francesca's little sacrifice to their new friendship.

And yes, they are all a part of the plan – of the preservation – the paying tourists, without whom the Duchesse could not manage to keep up the place, but whose constant presence is a barely tolerated encroachment, which, in the case of Francesca, becomes intolerable, after all. Is it because the Duchesse expected them to behave like *paysans*?

And try as Francesca might – to leave no footprint, as if they had never been – with Olga's help – Olga, of the Polish cleaning-lady origins – alas, it was not to be. The Duchesse would never visit their apartments, in any event, never see for herself how spotless they had kept their rooms, until after their departure, after the disaster, and would refuse to "receive" any one of Francesca's phone calls of entreaty.

So Francesca never got to lay the apology, nor reparations at the Duchesse's feet. Instead, the Duchesse simply confiscated their American funds, the funds Francesca had brought for the entire month, and simply bolted the doors to the other partner, who arrived the next day, fully unaware of what had happened – her entry, and that of her guests, equally barred.

No intercession on the part of the senior partner could avail. Guest though he had been for the past four summers, his bicycles and *cuisinart* now likewise seized in her turrets, the Duchesse would not take his second call.

She accused you of doing crude things in her forest... I know that is not you. I know you are a lady of Loretto, would not permit your son to defecate in her woods, nor would you ever do that...

It was not simply a question of the mirror...

"I did not come all this way to spend every day beside a pool," Francesca complains to her husband.

"I'm content with just this. Why can't you be? Why can't you just relax?"

"We're only forty minutes from Paris. Can't we at least hop a train? Marco travels well. He'll be happy anywhere we are."

She had a Mothercraft portable potty. There would be no regression for Francesca's son, as with Alessandra, whose parents had clapped her back in diapers for this trip.

"I have the perfect suggestion for what ails you."

"Nothing *ails me*," Francesca had lied, for, in fact, her panic attacks had begun again, in the night, and then chased her as she tried to work them off, jogging about the grounds...

"Lower your expectations..."

Diminished expectations had been what marrying him was all about – an unbearable loneliness of being, that she would never meet the man who would cherish her for who she was, that he, after all, was at least *easy* to be with, or so it had seemed at the time. She hadn't foreseen how arduous it could be to claw one's way out of a collapsing house, to constantly be picking through salvage for the necessities of life, what was left after the latest storm, the latest lawsuit, like the one she had most recently defended before departing for France. They had moved house, ten days before this holiday, and she'd sat ten Hamiltons (her husband's people) down to dinner, the day before travel – roast beef and

Yorkshire pudding – a feast spread out on the harvest table with the bone china she and the nanny had washed before the move, a feast which she had been unable to eat. Only she knew of the injunctive order that her senior partner had negotiated to be lifted, briefly, to enable the two real estate closings, before being transferred to Francesca's new home. Like a stain on the white lace tablecloth – this cloud against her title. It meant she could not sell, or even finance, without having to deal with her husband's creditors.

Her son slept in the sumptuous room off the Château's dining room, separated from theirs by a long corridor that would have befitted a boudoir farce. Nightly, she settled Marco and read him to sleep, until she heard his gentle breathing, while David and Zachary conversed, and Olga did the dishes, as Francesca had cooked the meal. Then Francesca would slip out of bed, and travel down the inner corridor that divided their rooms from the outer hallway that dissected the suites on opposite sides of the Château. Olga's and David's rooms faced the mirror lake; Francesca's and Zachary's looked out upon the gardens. She would lie still, listening to the voices of David and her husband that carried from the open window of the dining room, to her open window… and wait.

What courage did it take this toddler son – to face the length of that corridor, alone? Nightly, she would find relief in the sound of Marco's little feet hitting the floor from the high perch of his canopied bed, running wordlessly down the corridor toward their room where, in silent choreography, his father would scoop him up and deposit him into Francesca's open arms, then retreat to the other room, where father could better sleep out the night into the late mornings, uninterrupted, while Francesca and son would take their little boat on the mirror lake, or sit together in the swings, with inarticulate loneliness, at dawn.

On one of their walks, far away from the Château, Marco announced that he had to go *poo-poo*, and Francesca, looking around, walked with him deeper into the woods, found a low-hanging branch, looked around to ensure that no one was about, and removed the portable Mothercraft potty from her knapsack – proud of her own resourcefulness.

That afternoon, as every afternoon, they all congregated at the pool, David's Olga and Francesca's husband finally emerged from their sleep, Francesca and David ready for their first glass of wine – "tonic" as David called it – to chase the afternoon's heart-of-darkness.

"Paris is only forty miles from here. Can't we at least go to Paris?"

And so, to try to placate her restlessness, Francesca's husband suggested a drive. And sometimes motion did help.

In the back seat, beside her son, Francesca looks out at the countryside, the long avenues of regal trees alternating with farmlands, little villages. After hours of driving, it all begins to look alike.

"Where are we going?"

"Leave it to me; it's a surprise. Do you have to control, everything?"

So Francesca sits back, and sings to her son. Eventually, they arrive.

It is an outdoor restaurant in the middle of nowhere. They are the only patrons of the place. Francesca is charmed. They sit under the mature trees at a metal table. The owner spreads a cloth as her husband orders a rich burgundy, assorted cheeses and fruits. The proprietor returns to their table with a tiered platter, compliments of the chef, its three layers flowering with shrimp, little snails, and assorted seafood – no doubt about to go bad.

Seeing the lavish display, Marco bursts into song: "Happy birthday to you…" They all laugh. It is indeed an occasion. Francesca claps her hands together, as does her son. She is suddenly deliriously happy, abandoned at this exquisite moment, the unexpected gift of this afternoon.

"Are you all right to drive?" Francesca asks Zachary.

"We haven't far to go."

He pulls out of the restaurant parking lot, round one corner, and they are there, at the locked gates of the Château du Marais. He laughs at her realization, the dismay on her face. They have driven around in circles, only to land right back at the gates of the Château. He has managed to delude her, yet again. His laughter, like the one the morning after their wedding, when at breakfast he had lit a cigarette. Fool that she was, she believed him when he told her he had quit. Or, the day after their return from Jamaica, when she found the marijuana he had smuggled across the border – no *souciance* for the potential implications for his license to practice law, his wife, or their son… Laughing at the fish hook in her cheek, at her "trout look," as he is fond of calling it.

The eyes and ears of the Duchesse must have been everywhere. How else could the Duchesse know that Olga had purchased fireworks to celebrate Bastille Day? How else know about the defecation in her woods?

The fireworks were to be David's and Olga's gift to them for this holiday – a night's entertainment to be viewed from the open window of the dining room after dark.

One of the Duchesse's servants arrived at the door of their apartments: "Here, at the Château, we do not celebrate Bastille Day. Here, at the Château, there will be no fireworks."

The property quickly passed from Le Maître to a young widow. Madame de la Briche, who organized country festivals for the peasantry. 'We set large tables in the parkland alleys,' she recorded in her diary. 'The only expenses for a charming day, full of gaiety and good-will, were the cakes and spice breads, the wine, and the violinists for dancing.' Her generosity was happily rewarded, for Le Marais was left untouched during the Revolution.

It was not simply a question of the mirror.

Francesca is cleaning their apartments, using the vacuum cleaner Olga has located in a servant's cupboard. The cord is extended the length of their bedroom, and Francesca is working toward the master bathroom, and is in front of the full-view, stand-up and adjustable mirror, when her son bursts into the bedroom with his father, his arms extended toward her, little legs pumping. Francesca watches, as if in slow motion, at the obstacles between herself and the child; she tries to swing the cord in her left hand like a whip, away from his pumping feet, just as his left foot hooks the cord and hurtles him forward, a flailing Icarus, flying with his hands outreached toward the mirror. Francesca hurls herself toward her son and catches him, in midair, but not before his little hands contact the mirror and send it hurtling backward, toward the tiled floor of the bathroom. From where they roll on the carpet, her arms and body shielding him, she looks up in time to see the disaster as it unfolds – impact of the wood frame, the bounce, the shattering of the antique mirror into a thousand pieces.

The collateral shatterings to follow:

The business David founded, stolen by his partner while they were away in France.

David's oppression lawsuit, which will eventually bankrupt David and Olga, beginning with the collapse of their retirement funds.

Zachary's bankruptcy.

Then his suspension by the Law Society.

Their marital separation, when their son is only six.

David and Olga's home – lost to the trustee in bankruptcy, when David and Olga become unable to pay their debts as these become due. (Only the contents survive, whisked into some relative's barn, to be hidden under straw.)

The old Pontiac Sunbird that Francesca lets David and Olga use, then needs, herself, for her own salvage operations.

"I'm sorry, Olga. I'm so sorry. He's not giving me any child support. You can either pay me or give it back, so I can sell it elsewhere."

Olga sends David with the money.

At the hand-over meeting, Francesca says, "You know, he's got a woman – already."

"You mean the Brenda woman?" David says. Until that moment, Francesca had only suspected. The name registers like a slap.

"I'm so sorry," David says, when he sees the impact.

The sale of the old Pontiac to David and Olga saved her a few weeks of groceries. It cost Francesca their friendship.

Good memories? Such had been their denials and delusions at the time that, years later, she has blocked out even the fact of this book, how it came to be in her library.

Francesca gets up quietly from in front of the fireplace of the house she managed to salvage. She gets up quietly – lest she waken the sleeping son who is moving from boy to man even as he sleeps, moving out of her protection. She goes to search her cabinets for the Armagnac with which to marinate the cavities of her pheasants to be flamed with the cored, peeled, and thickly sliced apples.

While she is in the kitchen, the Christmas tree pitches forward – a matter simply of timing, the unbalanced weight of decorations. She listens frozen, with her hand on the kitchen cabinet, to the sound of shattering.

They collide just outside the door to the kitchen. She blocks her son's bound into the front room, with his size 10 bare feet. Shattered bulbs are everywhere. They stand, surveying the wreckage. Water bleeds from the base of the tree and across the surface of the hardwood. A photograph floats free in the river toward her.

It is of herself – standing pregnant and waiting in front of their first Christmas tree. She picks it up. Her eyes stare into her eyes, across twenty-one years. It was there all the time. Even this. Nothing to do with the mirror, his future or her own.

"Does your Dad ever talk about the time we stayed in a castle?"

"Dad never mentions the past."

"I found a recipe for pheasant, while you were sleeping. I'm making pheasants New Year's Day."

"Cool."

"We stayed in a castle, with David and Olga. They had this little girl, Alessandra. She loved to kiss you, under the table. We were always finding the two of you, embraced. Do you remember any of it?"

"I remember a bat. You hid under the blankets with me, until Dad chased it away. You were really afraid."

"I forgot about the bat. I was that... *afraid*."

"Dad asked me, once, if you still kept in touch with them. I told him 'no.' He said that was a shame."

The apples will have a sweet, peppery taste. The recipe will turn out well, in the end. Strong, peasant roots that she has, Francesca always ensures they eat well. It is not about the food, anyway, but the company. Francesca may not have kept in touch, but she thinks of Olga every time she eats the gristle, which is every time she makes chicken soup, and of David, whenever she sees a Pontiac Sunbird. They are there, just as she is, in every mirror.

POWERFUL NOVENA
OF CHILDLIKE
CONFIDENCE

"Il mio mistero è chiuso in me."
> —From "Nessun Dorma," *Turandot*,
> by Giacomo Puccini

We will not all die, but we will all be changed…
> —*1 Corinthians* 15:51

PORCH STORIES

Mary Giovenazzo gives Francesca the plastic card upon which the Powerful Novena is written, and announces that her first-born, Elizabeth, will be at table this Christmas, staying a month. "Thank you, Mary, Jesus and Joseph. Thank you, for listening." It is one of those gift days of a Canadian Indian summer in late fall, where an unexpected sun tries to melt the cold from the air. Francesca and Mary sit on the Giovenazzo front porch, sipping rye on the rocks, sharing women stories. Francesca is in love with the eldest of Mary's sons, Vince.

"I never forgave Gugli that one," Mary says, meaning Guglielmo, her late husband, and "that one," meaning his forcing their sixteen-year-old daughter, Elizabeth, to marry the Maltese man who had impregnated her. "He sat there, where you're sitting, now, and I sat here, where I am today…"

The women cover a lot of history this day – Francesca's concerns for her own teenaged son, child of her own failed marriage. Mary talks of her own failure to comprehend "why?" – why did Vince's wife leave him with her little kids? Why this, and why that – the pain of perplexity unloosened by rye.

"They had such beautiful children together, and I know my Vince was working hard for her and the kids. He got that from Gugli. He was a hardworking man, my Guglielmo, and a hard man sometimes to live with. I know there weren't other women. Vince told me himself, and I believe him, my son. He's a loyal type, you know. I'll just never understand what she saw in that other man. Have you seen him? There isn't anything wrong with my boy, is there?" Mary shoots Francesca a sudden glance, and Francesca reads her fear. Francesca has a private thought of Vince, pulling her toward him one morning at the Tuscan country home where they had stayed, this summer past; Francesca had known the groundskeeper's wife would be watering plants on the terrace beneath them, and had urged Vince to wait. "She only understands Italian," Vince whispered as he nuzzled her from behind, making Francesca laugh in a way that there was no mistaking their meaning.

"Oh, Mary," Francesca assures Vince's mother, "he's a beautiful man. He's a good man. There's nothing wrong with your son, in *that* or any other department." She laughs, and Mary, taking her at her meaning, seems relieved. Francesca, this afternoon, is so in love with Mary's son that the pain of Mary's porch stories seems mercifully removed.

"No, I'll never forgive Gugli that one."

The pregnant Elizabeth, gifted and intelligent, had been taken from the private girl's school education Guglielmo had worked so hard to give her. There had been other options, and Mary researched these all and advocated each before her husband. One was a home run by the nuns, where Elizabeth could have continued in school. Another was Mary Giovenazzo herself raising Elizabeth's child — just one more in the family. This was Mary's preferred choice. Abortion, of course, was never considered – not for this devout Catholic family. Marriage had been Guglielmo's choice.

"It broke my heart, the first time I met them, his parents. It broke my heart to see what kind of people Elizabeth was getting – rough and rude. A miner's son my Gugliemo may have been, but a mean man he was not. Not like the man she had to marry. I said, 'Let them live here – Elizabeth and her child. I'll raise them both, mother and son.' But Gugli would have none of it. And Gugli, *being the man,* forced them to get married. And I, *being the woman*, of course, I obeyed."

Mary shuffles irritably, refusing to absolve herself of any responsibility. Guglielmo may have forced marriage upon Elizabeth – forced her to marry the Maltese man who had impregnated her and who took marriage as a licence to abuse her for the next thirteen years – but it is Mary who has borne the responsibility, in her own books. Guglielmo was only doing what Guglielmo thought right; Mary *knew* it was wrong, and let it happen.

Then Elizabeth had made her own choice.

When the boy, John, was thirteen, she fled her marriage and went alone to Vancouver, and left the son behind with his father. She knew, *being the man he was,* her abusive husband would fight her for custody, and Elizabeth was running for her life. She couldn't handle the brutality in a different form. She relinquished the prize. She went to work at a battered-women's shelter. Her heart hardened like a stone against all men, but most especially her father. Even her brothers she saw through the darkened filter of her own truth. *I believe, therefore it is.* Might Elizabeth not also have seen her son, John, in the same light? For wasn't the son male, and didn't all men ultimately share the same fate – abusers all – according to Elizabeth?

Every time Francesca visits Mary at her house, she studies the black-and-white chalk portrait of Elizabeth over the fireplace mantel. She has no idea when this likeness was drawn. But it cannot be from before Elizabeth's marriage. The woman in it is too mature – a middle-aged woman. This must have been something Elizabeth sent back east – something to stare down the family in her absence. In the portrait, Elizabeth has hard, judgmental eyes.

Francesca has also often studied the photograph of Elizabeth's boy, John. A confirmation photograph, he stands in a graduation-type gown with a sash around his neck and the name "John" on the sash. He stands beside a woman. The first time Francesca sees it she remarks to Vince: "Elizabeth looks just like your mother Mary."

"That's because she *is* Mary," says Vince.

And then Francesca realizes: Elizabeth wasn't there. Elizabeth had not attended her only son's confirmation. Mary had stood in place of John's mother.

Francesca's own son also chose the name John as his confirmation name – not after any saint, not John the Apostle, not John the Baptist – but after his grandfather. Francesca prays the resemblance between the boys ends there.

John is much softer looking than the Giovenazzo men, although Francesca knows how gentle and tender her own Giovenazzo man can be. Whoever Elizabeth's son was or might have been, he was clearly conflicted – torn apart by his anguish. No one makes that irrevocable choice except out of unbearable pain. "The absence of God," was how the nuns defined Hell, the ultimate alienation – like exile by a parent. Like Elizabeth perched in Vancouver, at the end of the world, an entire country between her and her family. Such extremity. This pain, surely, was punishment enough. Yet, to add to it, in death, burial outside the gates, darkness overwhelming…

Mary goes into the house and returns to the porch with the "Powerful Novena of Childlike Confidence" to help Francesca with her son. She brings back with her the bottle of rye to refresh their glasses. Francesca's boy, whose beautiful voice has got him "imprisoned in a boy's school," is breaking his heart to be "sprung" from this imprisonment. Shortlisted for acceptance at a school of the arts, Francesca knows his desire has nothing to do with singing. Rather, a ratio of fifteen girls to every adolescent male is his motivation. It seems wrong, somehow, to use a Powerful Novena to increase the sexual odds.

Powerful Novena of Childlike Confidence

O Jesus, Who has said, "All that you
Ask of the Father in My Name, He will
Grant you," through the intercession of
Mary, Thy Most Holy Mother, I humbly
And urgently ask Thy Father in Thy Name
That my prayer be granted.

(Make your request and believe it will be answered.)

La Visitazione

The Tuscan country home where Francesca and Vince stay the summer before Elizabeth's Christmas visit is close to a church that houses a special painting – *La Visitazione* – near a Medici summer palace. When Francesca looks at Vince with "those eyes," Vince says: "One more church and I'm wearing a white collar and withholding my body." Yet he will drive those two hours for the love of her.

Alone in the church, Vince sits in a pew, like a hockey player in a penalty bench, while Francesca gazes at the painting. She gazes at Mary and Elizabeth, in profile, embracing, looking into each other's eyes. Waiting for them to speak, waiting for them to reveal their meaning, across centuries of silence, with the language of their creator almost lost, like faith itself. And then she sees it is a quartet of women, not two. For looking more closely at the obscured women just off at an angle, Francesca realizes the woman behind Elizabeth *is* Elizabeth, and the woman behind Mary *is* Mary, and what the artist Pontormo has done is give to Francesca their vision, what *they see*.

And these are Mary's eyes, so deep and still, and going back forever; and Elizabeth's eyes, so full of compassion, and love, and human tenderness. This is Mary, having walked all that way, pregnant with the Lord; and this is Elizabeth, her aged aunt, having thought herself sterile, who has conceived, and is full of John the Baptist, who is yet to be. And at the moment of this encounter, the child in Elizabeth's womb leaps.

She gave a loud cry and said: Of all women you are the most blessed, and blessed is the fruit of your womb. Why should I be honoured with a visit from the mother of my Lord? Look, the moment your greeting reached my ears, the child in my womb leapt for joy. Yes, blessed is she who believed that the promise made her by the Lord would be fulfilled.

Francesca feels a shiver of recognition and excitement that has her dancing before the painting, almost shouting out in the church, "Come here, Vince, this you've *got to see. You have to see this.*"

ON THE DEATH OF STARS

In the year Francesca's boy turns thirteen, mother and son travel to an observatory, near the northern

Ontario resort Francesca books to celebrate his birthday.

Inside the observatory, they look through the telescope at globular clusters, and also look at the ring left by a star, newly dead – the expelled gas forming a kind of cocoon surrounding the cinder of the dead star.

"The cloud around the cinder glows with different colours," says the female astronomer, "depending upon its distance from the dead star, chemical composition, and density."

The star, newly dead, through the telescope, reminds Francesca of a pregnancy test. Francesca is remembering, not her living son's pregnancy test, but the one that married her to his father–a little orange blob with a thick outer ring, evidence of a life she later miscarried.

"When stars die, they actually give birth to new stars. Stars contract as they age, draw their energy into themselves. When they explode, this energy is out there, transformed, and these exploded parts start to whirl. The expelled gases – a cloud or nebula of gases, such as nitrogen, hydrogen, helium, and oxygen – start to whirl faster and faster and adhere to each other and ultimately form new stars. *The energy does not disappear but transforms into new forms of energy.*"

"You should think really hard about this," she says to her son quietly, on the way home from the observatory.

"It's not such a big deal," her son replies. "It's obvious, when you think about it. It's like anything, when it dies, new life grows out of dead bodies, vines growing off rotted logs."

Francesca whispers: "You know, some parents love their kids just because they had them. I love you because you are you. I think you're awesome." In the dark, staring straight ahead at the road in front of them, her son says, "Back at you," closing the circle in which they used to orbit about each other and still sometimes do.

CONFIGURATION AT TABLE

Vince sits at the head of the table, where his father used to be. His mother, Mary, sits off to his right, closest to the kitchen. Francesca sits to Vince's left, opposite Mary. Francesca's son was to be at table, but is not. This Christmas day, Francesca's son has gone to his father. Francesca stacks her son's cutlery on top of his plate, clears the space in a nervous clatter. Elizabeth's eyes meet Francesca's across the table.

Vince summons: "*In the name of the Father, and of the Son...*" and everyone makes the sign of the cross, obedient to the call for grace.

It is a lively table. For someone who has lived in the desert until the day she reappears to her family, Elizabeth doesn't hold back her verbal punches. And as Elizabeth swings, Francesca feels Vince's body tighten itself. Francesca presses his foot reassuringly with her own, as if she could conduct and defuse some of this energy. She asks Vince if he will please get her another piece of ham, being closer to the kitchen. When Vince stands up with her plate, Elizabeth says:

"But Vince has never *served* anyone."

"But he helps me all the time," Francesca says. "Your brother is so caring of me," as Vince drops the plate with the ham in the kitchen. Vince looks stricken and helpless as he kneels to mop up the mess.

"When Vince was a kid," remembers Elizabeth, "he would never let anyone taste anything from his plate. I can't believe he's letting you spoon up those cranberries. If I so much as touched Vince's bowl of ice cream with a spoon, Vince would waste the balance..." She goes on and on, about this and that, seeking some place to land, and there is no safe place. No one dares say anything. Everything has the potential to explode. And what Francesca reads around the table is *fear*.

For her own boy, who is not with her, Francesca feels a sudden fear. *Mary, Jesus and Joseph, let no bad happen.*

Vince told Francesca how John had died. Vince had visited the very spot, and talked to a woman from the apartment building near the bridge, seeking answers. John had sought out his mother, at the age of twenty-six – left the father in Toronto to find his mother in Vancouver. Vince confessed to Francesca how, after the funeral, he had gone to a restaurant for a cup of coffee. There was no one in the restaurant – with its flamingo pink art deco – and booths with a mirror behind the serviette dispenser, salt and pepper and ketchup bottle. Looking out the window, with its neon-script sign, watching the odd person pass, Vince felt at the very end of the world. Alone in the restaurant, but for the man who ran it, nursing his cup of coffee, Vince wondered about his nephew at that terrible moment. What kind of courage would it take, what horror of misunderstanding or comprehension?

Vince tells Francesca that, at John's funeral, Elizabeth accused him.

"Abuser," she called him.

"Would you set the record straight on this one?" Vince turned to his then wife, "Say something."

But by then, everyone was screaming.

"You're no different than him" – *pointing to the Maltese monster, saying to brother, to father, what she could not say to her former husband.*

"You're not the only one who lost someone, here." *Vince tried to defend himself against his sister, "I lost a nephew."*

"I'll bet you beat her every night, too. It's better than sex, isn't it, Vince?"

"I was there at the house, when you abandoned John in Toronto. I was there to watch, while Ma was raising him. I was there for him, when you weren't. I'm here now. I'm here to mourn my nephew. I'm here for him. This isn't about you…"

"You're here for yourselves. You're all here for yourselves. You're all guilty. I forgive none of you."

Words from a place of crazed and incomprehensible pain.

They all returned to Toronto. All, except Elizabeth. Too many things said and unsaid. She lived, if at all, in self-imposed exile. Her mother, Mary, lived with the fracture and dissension of her family.

Does anyone leap for joy at Elizabeth's return? Does anyone think, "Blessed be thou amongst women, blessed be the fruit of thy womb?"

This Elizabeth Giovenazzo stayed with *this* mother Mary a month and then was gone. No one quite understands, amongst other things, why she came in the first place.

Ought a Powerful Novena ever be used to bring back the dead?

Who was she? *And she confessed...*

I am the voice of one crying in the wilderness... Between birth and death is only a span, and it will not be crossed except by tears. Then they wept together. Some say John wept so much that tears marked his cheeks.

Who was John? Who was Elizabeth? Whoever they were, Francesca prays, without confidence, that they be released from their suffering. Or at very least, be granted new lives – transformed energy, as do stars, when they die. That they get to collect bits of others about themselves, that they burn again, bright new little stars, not so alone in the universe.

ENTERING SICILY

Soon after we enter Sicily, my grandmother's story begins to inform what I see. I stare out the window at the slopes of hills as sensuous as the breasts of reclining women, hills planted at perilous inclines, with modern windmills now cresting these – not Nicolina Leone's Sicily at all. But I intuit from the walled estates, the outcropped single-room dwellings that still offer respite from the midday sun, what it must have been to be the daughter of a *padrone,* the husbandman who oversaw the owner's lands and labourers in the absence of the titled owner in Palermo or Messina.

"I can still see my father's house," Nicolina said the last time I saw her alive. She was feeling blindly for her piece of chicken on the plate. It would be my last visit with her and the aged aunt in whose home she then lived. Nicolina stared into the distance behind memory. "I see my father's house…"

My grandmother described her father's house, how she and her stepmother had brought food and wine up to the second storey, where only the men ate at the long table.

"My lips never touched the glass."

"Well, you're never too old to learn," I said. Astonishingly, my grandmother smiled and took a sip from the shot glass of wine I insisted on pouring for her and placed in her hand. She was one hundred and three. That day she ate with appetite.

"You don't take photographs here, and you don't ask questions about Leones, Spataforas, or anybody else," Warren advises.

We are in Salemi – sister town to Vita, in Sicily. Warren has driven us out from Palermo, and we arrive in Salemi about 10:30 a.m. We head to a bar just off what seems to be the main square, and I order *panini* and *due espressi*, mindful of the time to make it to Vita before the siesta.

"Do you think we stick out?" Warren asks, being facetious.

He is wearing a Red Wings hockey jacket and is of a weight and presence that towers above the diminutive men in the bar. I wear a brown leather jacket and blue jeans with zippered pockets. But it is more than our clothing. I am the only woman at the bar. And we speak to each other in English. We are *stranieri*.

As we eat our *panini*, the old men of Salemi stare at us and we look back at them, looking back at us.

According to her own story, no one had ever loved Nicolina as much as her stepmother; nor had she ever loved another as much as that good woman. It wasn't always so. The adored apple of her father's eye, Nicolina looked upon the stepmother as usurper of her father's attentions. Nicolina was only three when her mother died falling off a horse with the unborn twins twisted in her womb, when her father remarried. Initially, Nicolina would have none of the stepmother, gave her a tough time. Until the day the stepmother placed her firmly in a tub of water and gave her a bath. While administering to Nicolina's body, in soap and water to the elbows and on her knees, she made a deal with her three-year-old stepdaughter.

Your father will always prefer you to me, but he needs me to help him take care of you. This can either work well for us both, or it can go really hard. It's your choice. Respect me, and I will love you, always. But if

you choose to go against me, it will go very badly for us
both. The choice is yours.

How did she figure it out, in those days before psychologists, to position it thus before a rebellious, fiercely intelligent and manipulative three-year-old – to give Nicolina the choice?

"Think of the times," I say to Warren, "what it must have been like – a woman alone. You either married or you starved, and what a dangerous business it must have been in those days, keeping the love of a tough man."

"That tastes good," says Warren to the owner of the bakery we have entered in Salemi, to get directions to the sister town of Vita. The slender owner, comprehending, laughs with her mouth stuffed full of *cannoli*, and signals with her free hand toward her shelves, palm outstretched and welcoming, as if to say, *Please, help yourselves*. While Warren delights his eyes with the fresh pastries, I am fascinated by the sculpted and lacquered breads in varying designs. I purchase two clusters of bread grapes – one for my mother back home in Canada, one for my own harvest table.

Nicolina sings to me, clapping the hands of my then infant son…

> *Batti manini ca veni Papà*
> *porta cose e sinni va*
> *porta nuci e cassateddi*
> *pi manciari ai figghi beddi.*
> *Porta mennuli e castagni*
> *pi accurdari a chiddi granni.*

Here comes Papa, so clap these hands
He brings good things, all from the land;
He brings you nuts and little cakes,
Melons and fruit to make you great.
Almonds and chestnuts, sweet cheese for this day
A kiss for Mama, and then he's away.

"My little Vito," keened Nicolina, "I see my Vito…"
Don't say it, I think, don't tell me that story, not while holding the hands of my own infant son…
"He used to run to me, and pound his little chest. I gave him life. I could not give him breath."

"My great-grandfather had to be tough, or he would have starved. They all would have starved along with him."

And Nicolina's father was tougher than most – a *padrone* of another's lands.

The stepmother, herself widowed, came to the marriage with a son, Paolo, with whom Nicolina later fell in love when her time came to discover love. Her father forbade this love, married her instead to Spatafora who would eventually take her to Canada – breaking three hearts in the process – four, if you included his own.

From the hilltop town of Salemi, I see a vineyard of Nero d'Avola grapes, and wonder if this might have been part of the very lands my great-grandfather oversaw?

I must have heard it at my aunt's table – the aunt who was taking care of my aged grandmother. My grandmother was only sixteen at the time when my great-grandfather forced her to marry the man who would become my grandfather – Rosario Spatafora. In those days, when a man wept for weeks without explanation he was put into a mental institution. Nicolina had to wait until she was of legal age before she could sign him out – her sensitive young husband – the man who had crossed the ocean four times, the man her father had forced her to marry. Rosario's fifth crossing would be his last – with

Nicolina, then twenty-one. He would never return again.

"Yolked to a sick man... On my wedding night they gave me a bowl of water and vinegar, with a cloth. *O Dio,* married to a sick man..."

"Why didn't you tell me that my grandfather had a nervous breakdown?" I challenge my mother when I first learn of my grandfather's incarceration in a mental institution.

"What difference would it have made?"

"It would have helped explain."

"Explain what?"

Explain why Nicolina had no children the first five years of her marriage, why they all came afterward – in Canada. Explain me, possibly, to myself. Explain that motion sickness of the soul, what happens when you lose your center of gravity, travel too many distances too many times, too far from home – the unbearable suffering of the displaced person. Explain how I myself had felt, after Vancouver, the panic attacks – the most recent of these in Agrigento, in the Valle dei Templi – as Warren slept through the siesta and I clung to his breathing body, as if to *home*.

"So when the guys back at the coffee shop ask me how I spent my vacation, I'll tell them I wandered around graveyards." The coffee shop to which my Warren refers is Messina Bakery in Toronto. The coffee shop in Salemi was called Extra Bar.

The names: Spatafora, Leone, Agueci, Caradonna, Gandolfo, Pedone, Bascaglia, Gucciardi, Pace – vaguely familiar – names heard in my parents' stories of growing up around Clinton and College, in Toronto.

Spatafora. Of those who remained, they must have done all right for themselves, because there is a Spatafora mausoleum, in the newest part of the Vita graveyard.

None of the graves are old enough to be recognized by my parents as contemporaries of Nicolina, though the names are shared. She arrived in Canada just at the turn of the century, in 1906. Still, I take pictures.

GUCCIARDI MARIA   SPATAFORA MICHELE
VED. SPATAFORA   FU GIUSEPPE
*26-9-1881 + 2-12-1974   *25-10-1872 + 14-9-1958

"How many churches can there be in a town this size?"

The one church I am seeking – the one where my grandmother caused to have a plaque made in honour of her father's memory – I cannot find. It was probably bombed during the war, or lost in an earthquake. The only church we do find, and this before the siesta, is closed. The founding dates on the plaque outside its central door are beyond the dates of my grandmother's story.

"She was running after her nephew," my mother says. "I think her name was Anna, my real grandmother, the one who died, falling from a horse."

"What do you mean, *running after?*"

My mother explains: "Her husband's brother had a son, Vito. I guess he was a young boy, and his father used to beat him. They were tough customers in those days."

"Who, my great-grandfather?"

"No, his brother. But they were both tough customers. Vito ran away. Your great-grandmother, Anna, I think her name was, she got on a horse and chased after him, to bring him home. But she was pregnant, and fell off the horse, and that's how she died."

The town of Vita feels dead. It is more alive in the graveyard, above the town, where at least there are the pictures of its former inhabitants. With its rows of mausoleums, the Vita graveyard mimics the society of the town below, but on a miniature scale. And what hard faces stare out of these stones – as if not a single life had been happy.

Survivors of Vita Bascaglia have planted roses. Three buds burst pink, red and salmon to adorn her tombstone – monument of a life lived from 1898 to 1973. I think of the profusion of roses that bloomed around Nicolina's porch – the scent of summer so heady I'd feel drunk on my tea and my grandmother's porch stories.

Nicolina Leone returned to Vita in Sicily only once, for the death and burial of her father. She stayed almost a year, accompanied by her two small children, infants under five. She returned to keep vigil over her dying father and then, upon his death, remained for some time longer to be of comfort to her stepmother. And when Nicolina left Vita that final time – after having seen her father honoured with the tomb built with the money she had inherited from him – she left in a *carretto tirato da un cavallo*, her stepmother walk-running at the wagon's side. For miles, the stepmother accompanied them on foot. And Nicolina would stop the driver and get down and embrace the old woman, and the old woman would embrace Nicolina and the children she was certain never to see again. And for as many miles as Nicolina could bear, it went on like this, with the old woman beside the cart, weeping, and the cart stopping and everyone getting out, embracing, weeping, and back in again – struggling to say goodbye in a way the adult women knew to be final. Until at last the old woman stood still in the dusty road and watched, as they passed out of sight on the road *direzione* Palermo, from there to Naples, to the boat that would take them across the ocean, forever.

Forever. Never again. Not ever, in this lifetime. How do you do that – part – when you know you will never, ever, see the object of your love again?

The story of Nicolina's own death: the aged aunt took my grandmother and herself to an old folks' home. The aunt stayed in the assisted living wing, while my grandmother was put in with the really decrepit – those with dementia and Alzheimer's, and those who couldn't "do for themselves." Nicolina, although blind and deaf, had all her mental faculties. She protested in not-so-subtle ways. *"Perché sono qui?"* "Why am I here?" she would proclaim at the dinner table, where her dinner companions were strapped to their wheelchairs and stared, disinterested, at their Wonderbread food. Ever an elegant woman, whose father had returned from Palermo with parasols and bolts of fabric she turned into the fashions of the day, Nicolina would break wind at this last dinner table, to lend emphasis to her protest. There was no one here with whom to make a deal. At night, she called out names – of those she had loved, or who had loved her. Sadly, my mother's name was not among them.

Three days before she died, Nicolina had her last bowel movement. She washed her private parts – never permitting anyone to touch these. She lay on her bed, and folded her hands neatly across her chest. She summoned Aunt Vitina to shave her – Vitina, named after the town and the dead little boy, Vito, who had come and gone before her. Nicolina willed her own death. The vanity with which she had lived her life ensured her face would be hairless in its final display. In fact, Nicolina had looked resplendent in death.

"Don't worry," Warren says to me, in the car, just outside the graveyard of Vita. "I will find someone to shave you."

"Forget the shave. It's about the picture on my grave…"

Tough. They were all tough – tough, as in hanging two loads of laundry while in labour with your first child.

Tough, as in being forced to marry your father's choice.

Tough, as in burying your child – named after a town in Sicily that means "life."

Tough, as in pretending not to recognize your youngest child, my mother, your daughter, while she was washing your face during those final three days – "Francesca? Who?" When you well knew who she was – lucid to the last moment. Because love did not exist in your vocabulary, then, not ever again, after your tough father married you to the Spatafora who took you to Canada, not ever again after your stepmother died.

Forever. Never again. Not ever, in this lifetime. How do you do that – part – when you know you will never, ever, see the object of your love again?

"Ma, if it came to a choice between hearing it from my mother and hearing it from my own child, I'd rather hear it from my child" – words I said to my mother after Nicolina's death, when my mother could not get over her grief that Nicolina had died without acknowledging her – whose hand it was that held the wash cloth: *" I love you, Ma, I love you."*

Vito. Vita. Vitina.

Names on stones. Lifetimes reduced to a single story line. "Anna, I think her name was. She died falling off a horse, the unborn twins twisted in her womb." Names on stones. Names, ultimately, that identify nothing – a slow relentless vanishing...

"Take a picture," Warren says, as we leave Vita. Obediently, I turn around in the car and stick my camera out the window, backwards. The sign is rusted and bears the symbol for "no horns." The sign says:

VITA
BENVENUTI A
WELCOME TO
BIENVENUE A
WILLKOMMEN IN
VITA

I make my Warren toot the horn in defiance and affirmation. As always, he obliges me. He has no idea why I ask him to honk, looks at me surprised and uncomprehending. Yes, blow it – again – hard. Lean on that horn! Sound the horn for those who can no longer hear it. Yes, sound it, for me.

GOING WHERE, EXACTLY, WITH THIS MOTION?

From: Timo [Timo@hotmail.com]
Sent: Monday, November 9, 2009 1:17 PM
To: Francesca [Francesca@hotmail.com]
Subject: Re: Going where, exactly?

Franny:

I'm happy you made it safely through the long trip and back.

You will live your trip for years to come; that is the way they are, and is it not why we make them? Events, even small ones, are recalled and pondered over. Sometimes in thought, I find myself in the back streets of Juarez due to the news coverage. Other times musing something quite pleasant, a sunny stroll at the end of the peninsula in Charleston, South Carolina. Charleston is a rare piece of America, in that it is worth visiting. Already almost three years old, these were my events around the time when my granddaughter, Gia, was born.

November begins the season of reflection, unless travel takes its place, and this year it did not – so fireworks near English Bay were revisited, as were dining and dancing in Toronto... Maybe you and I ought to have done more of it; in any case I've also tried since, and there is shake left in these old legs. Sounds live forever in the mind; it is wealth to each of us to feel and love them, old melody and new.

I've also shelved the vodka, am working on a calorie counting diet so as to gain back some trousers hanging in the closet. Banal is the nature of honest reality, lies are much more pleasant.

Do write

Timo

From: Francesca [Francesca@hotmail.com]
Sent: November 9, 2009 10:35 PM
To: Timo [Timo@hotmail.com]
Subject: Re: Going where, exactly?

Timo,

You've shelved the Vodka, and I'm onto my 2nd Grappa for the night. I peeled back from 123 lbs, (my full-term pregnancy weight) to 118 lbs within two weeks of the return, and this evening I am down to 115. So, I'm celebrating with Grappa.

Living trips for years to come: Many years ago, I remember Adam saying to me: Would you rather have a trip or a couch? At the time, incredibly, I would rather have had a couch, because I thought we really needed one – to sit on. But we never actually stayed together long enough to sit anywhere. You are absolutely right about trips, living in the mind, and that among other things giving us our content and meaning. I still remember Avignon, brushing my hair at an open window, and the pigeons, and thinking of you, in the convent room with six student cots that my mother and I had rented for the night – our rogue trip away from Paris with nothing but knapsack and fresh underwear and our toothbrushes between us. I am sure I was beautiful then, at 26. I am also sure I worried about my weight, the French brie, in that clingy dress I wore at the time, because it was washable and would dry overnight. I am still there, somehow, in that open window, as the sunsets, and my hair, still wet, and that dress still clinging.

This trip. There is one picture. Me, at 57, on the temple ruins. In blue jeans, white shirt, thin air-holed sneakers, no socks – gamin style. Sicily. Agrigento. It is a picture of being perfectly at home – notwithstanding the panic attack I alone know I had that very day, over the siesta. It is me, in hope, at the sunset, with Sicilian sun on my face, leaning toward something, and so very expectant – joyous. (I had finally, of course, fit into my jeans, after denying myself pasta. But no, not for sure, because my white tailored shirt is out, and probably, my top blue jean button is open, under the shirt.) There is a moment, there, where to my eyes, anyway, I look absolutely beautiful. Unabashedly so, in the way I know, at the age of 104, looking back on me then, I'll think – damn, you were gorgeous – like the way I know I must have been in Avignon, at 26, even without a camera.

Do you ever want to weep for *who you were?*

I will continue to try to celebrate it all, including the detours, still believing that it is all about the journey. I will defer arriving, for as long as I can, for as long as I can distract the conductor; and when, eventually, I must get off, I will look back, however briefly – at that woman in the window of a convent school in Avignon, and at that woman half seated on the ruins in Agrigento, leaning to the left, poised on her piano finger tips, going where, exactly, with this motion – this *élan?* And I will think – that I have known this, that I lived to see and feel and taste and have this, however briefly, that these moments hap-pened to me, and I will finally understand what *it* is...

Franny

TRAVEL STORIES

In Memoriam Joseph Hoare
October 1, 1940 – October 29, 1997

In a panel above the altar of Saint Michael's Cathedral, Christ is a teenager in the temple talking with teachers. My friend Joseph, in his last weeks of life, told me that as a Saint Michael's choirboy he used to stare at this panel. He took comfort in the biblical story, as he prepared for his last journey. Joseph was a great traveller and gourmand. He worked as a gourmet editor of a Toronto magazine. When he phoned to tell me he had stomach cancer, I asked him if he had contemplated the ironies – Beethoven with his deafness, Milton on his blindness, "You…" "Well," Joseph said, "I would hardly put myself in such company," and we laughed, before we cried.

He said he was thankful for the kind of disease that was giving him time to get his house in order.

"Joseph, when you get to where you are going, will you promise to get a message across? Is there a destination on the other side of this journey?"

He promised he would, asking a promise in return. "Tell my mother. She need not sorrow. I am not lost. I was packed and ready for this journey."

And his parents went every year to Jerusalem, at the solemn day of the Pasch.

And, when he was twelve years old, they went up into Jerusalem, according to the custom of the feast.

And having fulfilled the days, when they returned, the child Jesus remained in Jerusalem. And his parents knew it not.

And thinking that he was in the company they came a day's journey and sought him among their kins-folks and acquaintance.

And, not finding him, they returned into Jeru-salem, seeking him.

And it came to pass that, after three days, they found him in the temple, sitting in the midst of the doctors, hearing them and asking them questions.

And all that heard him were astonished at his wis-dom and his answers.

And seeing him, they wondered. And his mother said to him: Son, why hast thou done so to us? Behold, thy father and I have sought thee sorrowing.

And he said to them: How is it that you sought me? Did you not know that I must be in my Father's house?

Was it the idea of his father's house that had so comforted Joseph? The idea of returning home, or being home, or never having left? The way we feel at the end of a journey – glad to be home? Isn't that one of the main reasons we take holidays? To return?

I am convinced that Joseph is an angel. In this energetic capacity, he helped my son's admission to Saint Michael's Choir School, which Joseph knew this mother desired so much for her boy. So for three years, I stared at the same panel of Christ in the temple, as my son, my sacrificial lamb, sang as if no one were listening, for the greater glory of God and the will of his mother.

The summer before my son's eighth grade, when he was twelve, the voice that got him "imprisoned in a boy's school" then "sprung him loose." He sang his way into the Cardinal Carter Academy for the Arts, fifteen girls to every boy – from choirboy to rooster in a henhouse. That summer of his coming of age, mother and son took a Mediterranean cruise.

Master Marcus,

O, sweet pea, comme dice la tua Momma.

I am at the Hotel Flora, in Venice, where once stayed your mother, writing what will be your very first postcard. May you someday see Venice, as did your mother.

Ciao, Joseph.

As with all Joseph's rare postcards, in his distinctive calligraphic script, I have kept these, and used them to mark texts. This first postcard to my son I kept among my tour books of Italy, and found it again when I booked the cruise.

FLORENCE

We stand in front of Santa Croce. I say to my son: "If anyone had told me twenty years ago that, first, I would ever have a child, and second, I would ever be standing here again—"

"Ma. Ma," he cuts me short, "if you're going to cry, I'm out of here."

Expect nothing. That way you may be surprised, but never disappointed.

We have an hour-and-a-half to accomplish mission impossible in Italy: eat and shop.

"As soon as the Guide stops talking, follow me close. I've got my runners, and I won't look back."

My feet feel the cobblestones as if it were yesterday. Down this side street, *a sinistro, allora, a diritto* … We arrive at a little trattoria and take one of three tables, set in a box garden and sheltered under an umbrella. As we wait for the pizza with black olives and goat cheese, we drink Chianti.

"I'm happy," I announce. "Are you?"

"I'm happy," my son says conclusively, in this little custom of the feast, from all our holidays together, and at home in the breaking of bread for my favorite part of the day – dinner. Then he asks, suddenly nervous, "How will you find our way back?"

"Don't worry," I tell him. "I get lost in cars, never on my feet."

After the lunch, we buy a little box with a Florentine angel for my son's first girlfriend. He will give it to her upon our return home.

"Oh, my God."

"What, Momma, what? Are we lost – again?"

"No, son," as I take another wrong turn on the *way home, after the separation. "We're not lost. We just don't know where we are. There's a difference in that."*

And my only son sits back in the car seat, and sighs, with his little shoes swinging, figuring his mother has it all under control – will eventually find the way home. As she always does. We always get home, in the end.

"Here are the rules: You escort your mother to dinner, every night. You tour with me in the day because that's the point – introducing *you* to Europe. If you stay up all night, that's your choice. But, debilitated or no, you will disembark with me for shore at 8:00 every morning."

I figure where can he, a thirteen-year-old, go on a boat? That first night, throwing on blue jeans at 3:30 a.m., it takes me fifteen minutes to find him. He's talking with a group of teens in a lounge closed for the night. A crewmember vacuums the carpet. They're just talking. My son looks up startled as his mother fingers him off to the side. "But you said those were the rules. As long as I'm ready to disembark at 8:00 in the morning."

And he is.

But how could *I* be so free with my only son? What kind of a mother gives her child permission so prematurely?

Taste of Catalan Spain (Montserrat)

Travel through the fascinating city of Barcelona, stopping at the famous Gaudi's Sagrada Familia. Admire the beautiful Catalonian countryside en route to Spain's most spectacular natural phenomenon, the mountain of Montserrat with its spectacular rock formations. In the monastery of Montserrat you can see the holy icon of the Black Madonna, listen to the famous boys' choir and enjoy some free time to explore and take photographs. This is a major tourist attraction in Spain so it will be busy with visitors, especially in the summer months. After lunch at Montserrat you will return to Barcelona to continue your city sightseeing.

All the way up the mountain, my son sleeps. He passes through landscapes, his eyes closed. He is slouched and slack jawed on the bus, a wan smile, bedroom eyes, squinting into the Mediterranean sun. It is only when we return home, when the photographs are developed, that I will see him with the carnation in his teeth, the legs splayed, the blond "Bird" wearing the short skirt on his lap.

"Wait for me here, right here," I say as I disappear into the washroom. When I come back, he is nowhere to be seen. I run up the mountain path toward the monastery of Montserrat, where I catch up to a group from the cruise boat. "If you see my son," I say, "keep him with you." No one has seen him. I go with the group to the monastery, so I will know the way there and back after I find him. Up and down the mountain path I seek him, sending our family whistle over the cliffs, the one his father used before we separated, calling our son's name, who is only thirteen years old, after all. I am frantic as one half-hour slips into forty minutes, and an hour, not finding him, seeking him everywhere. What don't I think in that hour, that lasts eternity? Nothing, but the worst.

Son, why hast thou done so to us? Behold, thy father and I have sought thee sorrowing.

He is sitting on the curb near bus number two, his head on his arms, arms folded across his knees like crumpled wings, a garden angel.

I rouse him gently. "Do you have our water bottles?"

"They're on the bus. Sorry, Ma."

I am too relieved to reprimand. "No mind, hurry, we might yet catch the singing."

We run up the mountain path and enter the cathedral, where there is a wedding taking place. Right up toward the altar, just a few rows behind the wedding guests. The cathedral full of tourists prays the "Our Father." I count seven languages within close proximity. Then the choirboys usher in the priest. They sing a *Laudate Virgine*, and some other piece I do not recognize.

During the mass, he sits close to me, leans his big head on my shoulder, with its thickness of dark curls, my man-child, so that I think he must be sleeping again. But when the singing is over, he says that the British children squirming in front of us were rude.

"They have no idea how hard that piece is."

"How do you know?"

"We sang it at Saint Michael's."

I look at him, wondering. I say, a little too earnestly, "Do you understand how special this is? You are listening to a piece of fifteenth-century music, on a mountain in Spain. You *recognize* it because you sang it at Saint Michael's Cathedral in Toronto. You are a part of this. It is in you. The choir-boy will leave the school. But the school will never leave the choirboy. Wherever you are, you will always be home…"

You were lost. And now you are found…

I was never lost.

I was there, all the time.

We compared versions of the story. How it did and might have happened. He told me he had waited, *right there*, as instructed, his head down on his arms. When he woke, the voices all around him were speaking an unknown language. He figured I must have gone ahead, to look for him. He would wait in front of the bus. Sooner or later, we would have to return. He'd have gotten on the bus and returned to the boat, with the rest of the group.

"What would you have done, Ma?"

"I would have stayed on the mountain. I would have searched for you there until I found you. I would never have left without you. I realize I would probably have made the wrong choice, based on yours. Yours was the more practical."

Three years after my friend Joseph died, I woke one morning in panic. My son was with his father. It was the early years of our separation, and he was only six years old. I never got used to raising him half of the time. In the early hours of that empty Saturday morning, my first thought was, "Who will guide me? Who is there to guide me?"

I decided, that day, to organize a small library. Something kept sending me back to a particular book, a travel book with a green cover. I knew there was something in this book for me, yet I could not find it. Then, the third time I returned, again flipping through its pages, out fell a piece of paper. On it was the unmistakable hand of my friend Joseph.

"But tell me, Circe, who is to guide me on the way? No one has ever sailed a black ship to Hell."

"Odysseus," the goddess answered me, "don't think of lingering on shore for lack of a pilot. Set up your mast, spread the white sail and sit down in the ship!..."

Odyssey, X, 501-7

At Easter time, I kept my promise. I called Joseph's ninety-six-year-old mother. She wept into the phone. Mothers both, we wept together.

Perhaps it was the ordinary humanity of their fear that had so comforted my friend Joseph on his final journey – that to Mary and Joseph, Christ was still just a child, *their* child, after all, and capable of being lost. *How is it that you sought me? Did you not know...?*

Of course they did not know. How could they know? How could he think so? How could he have been so mindless of their care, of the fact that they had sought him sorrowing? He alone knew where he was, where he was, all that time. He alone knew he was safe. He had been *home*, all that time. Going about his Father's business in his Father's house. How could *they* know? *He* hadn't told them – mindless, errant teenager that he was.

CYCLING IN SARDEGNA

"Time is not a measure of distance," Francesca's son, Marco, says to her when she tells him the cycles last about four hours. It is the night before their first *giro* in Sardegna.

Time is not a measure of distance.

They lay on their single beds in the darkness.

"Don't worry about your mother," she says to her eighteen-year-old son, "This isn't a race. This is about you overcoming yourself. Don't look back. Put your foot on the pedal and go. I'll be somewhere behind you, bringing up the rear."

That he is in Sardegna at all with his mother is a gift. When Francesca told her own mother about her intentions to join this cycle group:

"I'd feel a lot better if I knew your son would be with you."

"Ma, I'm fifty-six. I don't think I need a chaperone."

"Just ask him." Francesca did. He said "Yes."

For not much longer now, will he accompany her. She knows this but has trouble accepting it, like Achilles's mother, Thetis. She knew this, even as she held the feet of her infant son, kissing those little feet. "Ah, you kiss his feet now," her husband had said to her, just years before their own separation. "These are the feet that will take him away from you."

They meet the other cyclists, Robert and Mie, at the airport, with their bizarre bike suitcases. Robert will spend their arrival night reconstructing these bikes.

"She is Japanese," says Francesca's son.

"How can you tell?"

"Her voice sounds like leaves falling. Don't you love the way she says his name?" Marco sings in a falsetto rise and fall, as if Mie's voice were a leaf being lifted by wind.

And Francesca wonders, could any man, even one named Robert, hear his name pronounced in such a way without feeling himself cherished?

"Aren't you going to try it out?"

Francesca feels like a circus bear on the bicycle: the handlebars too short, her legs not extending enough, wobbling all over. She gives up immediately before the horrified eyes of Robert and Mie. The bicycles Francesca and her son are trying to ride are rentals – hers with a small bell and a newspaper clip on the rear wheel – her son's with the handlebars set high – an antique touring bike with thick wheels – nothing like the under-arched handles, heads down, rear-up racers with which they'll be cycling.

"Fuck," Marco says, as they walk their bikes past the ghostly rows of those belonging to the Italian cyclists – clip-on shoes tucked neatly under pedals, dust-shrouds protecting the work of multiple oils and other forms of readiness. Hundreds of bikes, it seems to Francesca, losing count. To what has she committed them?

They deposit their rentals at the very back of the hotel storage tunnel.

"Forget the locks," her son comments cynically. "Nobody, but nobody, is going to steal these."

The room to which they are taken has one bed, a double.

"*Sono mamma. Mio figlio è uomo. Non è buono, un letto…*" she manages in her broken Italian. She is told in Italian to take the siesta, and afterward they will arrange a room transfer.

"Try not to disturb the bed," she says to her son as they lie back, side by side on top of the bedspread, knees bent over the end of the bed, still wearing their shoes. They pass seamlessly into sleep.

The next day it is raining, and the first *giro* is cancelled. Marco goes back to bed. Francesca hikes in the rain to the Grotto of Neptune with Dominique. Dominique is very French and feminine. She is the travel co-ordinator's right-hand woman. Dominique tells Francesca about her marriage:

"He was in love with his mother and, while I still cared for him and nurtured him, we could not continue in marriage. He had to love his oriental self." Dominique is not resentful at all at her own betrayal, when he did eventually find an oriental woman to love. "Love simply died." *Is there ever anything simple about the death of love?* Francesca wonders.

Upon their return from the cave of Neptune, the weather has broken. Broken or not, Francesca and son must get used to their rented bikes.

"Let's try Alghero. It's only fifty-nine kilometers."

Francesca's son will not wear his bicycle pants, insists on the ghetto basketball shorts. They struggle up the first hill and pause at an outlook.

"I can wait here while you go and get the shorts."

"If you mention the bike shorts one more time, I'm over-and-out. *O.A.O.* You read me?" Marco talks like he text-messages.

"Fine, you want sore balls, that's your choice. But what do I know? I'm just your mother."

She rags on him all the way; and he on her.

"Do you really have to pee, *again*? What is it with women? My eyes are now trained to look for coverage for my mother's ass."

"Don't make me laugh," she yells forward. "I'll lose what's left of my energy."

They make a lot of noise, mother and son.

There was something she had wanted to impart to her son in Sardegna. This, surely, isn't it.

Getting to Alghero is not an arduous cycle. What makes it feel difficult is being uncertain of the way, as with all roads never travelled. The signs are clear, but she and her son are alone, together, in a strange country, and there are long stretches where not even a vehicle passes. Relief comes with a signpost.

A cycle group from France clips by — about fifteen cyclists — with a unison clicking of gears and whirr of wheels. And for a brief while, Francesca and son keep pace with the French on their rented bicycles. It comforts Francesca that they can. Then, the French cyclists, like a school of fish, flash suddenly to the right.

"If they were going to Alghero, they've just gone the wrong way."

The sky looks ominous and desultory.

"I knew it," her son says when the French pass them again – this time, the walled city of Alghero within sight. The French give them a backwards wave, and Francesca feels a huge gratitude – whether at Alghero, or the acknowledgment of other cyclists, she isn't quite sure.

They are eating pizza, keeping guard over the bikes when the sky opens up and rain descends. After half an hour of watching rain, her son says, "There's no way this is going to end. Let's go."

The way back is arduous. She is fearful as they head out of the city in rush-hour traffic, in the rain. Her heart pounds. With Alghero at their backs, she has lost her sense of markers, simply struggles to keep up. Her son's bike, which is without a back fender, throws the wet dirt up his backside, even to his shoulder blades. She is just about to say it, when her son feels her thoughts…

"If you say *I told you so,* even once, I'm dusting you."

"You can't do that. I'm your mother. There's no way I'll make it back."

On the last stretch, he surprises her with his gentle coaching.

"C'mon, Ma. One more hill. It's all downhill to the hotel."

"Why are my legs burning?"

"You started too fast. Your heart can't pump enough blood to get a steady supply of oxygen to the muscles. Your muscles are probably burning glucose in the absence of oxygen. The waste bi-products are accumulating in the blood, and making your muscles feel on fire."

"How do you know this?"

"Ever watch the Olympics? Those athletes who have been at the front the whole race? You'll make it. Just keep pedalling. Past where you are is when the endorphins kick in."

He makes her stop at the side of the road, drink some fruit juice and eat the crust of their left-over pizza, which he'd had the forethought to save in their knapsack.

"There's only one way back to the hotel," he tells her. "You *have to do this.* Tonight," he orders, "you load up on carbohydrates."

And this hill turns out to be the last hill and they coast back to the hotel, Francesca on a float of euphoria and gratitude for her son.

Look at you – so strong... you don't know how really weak you are...

If anything ever happened to us...

You'll never be able to keep the house, without me...

Sell when you can; you are not for all markets...

He'll leave you in the end. He'll betray you. They all do.

You'll be alone.

Alone, and afraid...

All the voices through all the years – a choir of doubters, lending credence to her own.

The next day, the *giro* is again cancelled, as the rain continues. The organizers stick to their itinerary, announcing they will start with the third day's *giro* – the one that was to have been the last. It is 110 kilometers.

Mie and Francesca try to learn the salsa together, after the siesta and before the evening ablutions.

Mie's body is supple and rhythmic, as fluid as her voice. Francesca is a stranger to women dancing together, stiff and inhibited.

Mie tells Francesca that her deceased husband was an artist, twenty years her senior, with adult children unsupportive of their father's happiness with a younger woman. He was diagnosed with stomach cancer, and went quickly and in terrible pain. Alone in the depths of her grief, Mie was befriended by a street mutt, who pushed his furry head up under her limp hand as she sat on a chair in a public square of Florence.

"I named him Tosca. This name he accepted, as unconditional as his love."

Mie brought Tosca home to her Florentine flat. With the advent of Tosca, Mie's courage rallied, and she marshalled her deceased husband's sculptures for sale, over the opposition of his adult children. She staged a final sale in Florence, and with the proceeds, funded her way home with the dog. The bureaucracy was byzantine over Tosca's exit papers, the shots and quarantine.

"I knew my husband was watching over me, that he'd sent Tosca to guide and comfort me. Even this practical difficulty was to heal me. This is why I do not fear."

"Robert is a lucky man."

"Do you think so? Robert is a damaged man. I do not think he can trust a woman. He is full of fear. There is part of Robert that Robert cannot open. But so kind of you to say. I found Robert, the way Tosca found me. I held his hand. Robert has a choice to refuse. I wait. I still wait for Robert. Courage is not lack of fear. Courage is to choose, in face of fear. Now, Robert and I, we cycle together."

Mie laughs. Her laughter makes the sound of loss and leaves, rising and falling on a sonorous breeze.

"I wonder how Robert likes living with Mie's dead husband?"

Francesca looks carefully at her son. He is not joking. He seems to have accepted entirely that Tosca is the former artist, transformed.

That night at dinner, Robert says unexpectedly, "Son," reaching across the table. He places his hand, palm down, across the left hand of Francesca's son. "What you want to do in life is to avoid manipulative women. These drain your energy, pull you to earth, and leave you nothing but the memory of your own longing."

Robert has silenced the table. Dominique, Mie, Francesca all look at him. Marco simply pauses in the cutting of his lamb chop, Robert's hand on his hand.

Francesca thinks, *Thank you, God. Thank you for this messenger.*

At this moment, the hotel staff rescues them from their embarrassment – accordion, tambourine, and *la bella* Cristina – dressed in the traditional peasant costume of Sardegna.

"Ah, *la bella* Cristina," Francesca laughs. "My son has always had a sweet tooth for the tarts."

"Did you say anything to him?" Francesca's son says in her ear, beneath the music, as *la bella* Cristina approaches, tambourine hitting her seductively swaying skirts.

"About what?"

"About Emma?"

"Nothing. Nothing at all. I think he was talking about himself."

"I think so, too." Marco releases her.

The way Robert had reached across the table...

When she was pregnant with this child, Francesca had marvelled at the way her body had seemed a universal property – the man who came up to her on the dance floor, and told her he did not think she ought to be dancing *in her condition*. And the client, who touched her stomach with both hands like a basketball player before shooting a foul shot – shocked at the hardness of it. She didn't mind. It was almost as if it didn't belong to her, this protuberance, her own body no longer her own. At the hospital, the Indian nurse had commented, "This is a spiritual child, very spiritual." And those eyes, at three days of life, smiled up at her as if to say, *Relax, Ma. We're going to be just fine. You and me. It will all work out in the end. And in the end, there will be nothing more to cry about.*

That's the way Robert reached across the table – as if Francesca's son were communal property, belonging to them all, everyone's charge, everyone's care and responsibility.

Marco stands on the little stage after dinner, before the eyes of the cyclists and their families, takes a piece of paper from his blue jeans pocket, and snaps open the page, like a fan. When he speaks, it is in

Italian. Francesca is so surprised she almost doesn't recognize her own son.

"*La pillola del giorno dopo.*

Un bambino si avvicina alla mamma e dice:

'Mamma, mamma, a che serve la pillola del giorno dopo?'

La mamma risponde:

'A digerire i piselli del giorno prima!'"

After Marco finishes telling this joke that he'd been rehearsing all day with the staff – young men and women with whom he has only the language of youth in common – the crowd of cyclists bursts into laughter. Where has he found the courage to stand there and communicate laughter in a foreign tongue?

"*Hai capito?*" asks a cycling co-ordinator of Francesca. "You understand?"

She understands only that her son has been embraced by an instant and collective affection – for trying to speak in their language, for having the courage to do so. The next day, walking toward the spot where the tourists have clustered amid the rocks, he will be greeted like a celebrity with "Marco, *straniero.*" The young men will pinch his cheeks, or snatch out at his ankles, as he walks past. She understands that this is a necessary affection, beyond the love that she unconditionally will always give, and for which she, his single mother, alone uncomprehending of the joke spoken in Italian, feels enormously grateful.

THE GIRO

"La macchina antica è pesante," one of the cyclists says as Francesca walks her bicycle past, to take her place in the peloton. The Italian cyclist has reached out in a collegial way, but with critical concern, lifting the bike by the seat, as if to assess the situation.

"Sì, è pesante," she answers, smiling back at him.

The number pinned to her bike shorts is 168. There are about 200 cyclists, she figures. There are two motorcycles at the front, an ambulance and provision vehicle in the rear. The cyclists fill the circular driveway in front of the resort, where the sounds of the flapping international flags and conversation energize their beginning. Dominique will be riding in the ambulance. She takes Francesca's knapsack, which Francesca learns she is not allowed to wear. The organizers bark out the orders of the day on a megaphone, but in a jocular way, as if this is a Special Olympics. Francesca gives her son a swift embrace and heads to the back of the group.

The first seven kilometres feel like a meeting of the guys at the coffee shop. One cyclist chats on his cellular phone. Others talk among themselves. *This is O.K.* Francesca thinks, *this I can handle.* But then, in unspoken unison, they pick up the pace.

"*La signora canadese ha paura,*" one *guida* says on his walkie-talkie to another *guida* at the front, telling him to slow the pace. They have just descended the first hill. "*Non frenare,*" the *guida* yells to Francesca, who has used her brakes on the way down.

With every downward hill she visually locates her son, climbing up the other side. He is the youngest cyclist in the group, and that he is at the front has everything to do with fearless youth and brute strength – a young man in his physical prime, no sense, as yet, of physical limitation or mortality. He is wearing the cycle shirt that Dominique gave him, which shows his abdomen and shoulder muscles, his slender male waist. He sits upright with those touring-bike handles, his large feet in Adida running shoes, pushing the pedals, reminding her of the paws of a puppy golden retriever – so disproportionate in size to the clip-ons of the other cyclists. Son and mother are at opposite ends of the peloton, with the multicoloured flock in between.

One of the men at the back, riding with her, tries to urge her to move up into the group.

"*Non mi tocchi,*" she says to him, when he places his hand on her back to push her forward. "*Non sono l'ultima,*" she defends herself, "there's you and you," she indicates by pointing, not understanding that these men at the back with her are guides. One of them laughs. She hasn't understood, as yet, that the group can only go as fast as its weakest link, and that there are men in this group who will be deeply resentful of the fact that she, a woman – worse, a woman who has clearly never driven in peloton formation – is slowing them all down.

"*La donna indipendente…*" is added to the growing list of labels. "*La signora canadese…*"

About an hour into it, she overhears a conversation neither men expect her to understand – thinking language a shield. One bets the other *un milione di lire* that *la signora canadese* will not make it past 11:00 in the morning. She stops looking at the Sardegnan countryside.

She books it out to the centre line, and lets go, flying past the cyclists on their lightweight racing bikes. Francesca discovers the joy of letting go, that her *macchina antica* can compensate with its heaviness on the downward inclines. And because she has trained on a mountain bike, her *macchina pesante* actually feels light. It has been as if she has trained jogging with weights.

When she joins the other Canadians, still breathless and on the outside perimeter, Mie encourages her to accept the assistance of the "pushers." Mie tells her that on her first cycle, the guides had placed her in position where she was able to find her second wind. Robert counsels her as to how she can loosen the tension in her shoulders and neck, by being more buoyant with her grip on the handles. Robert also worries about Marco's leg extension, which seems off balance in the right leg. "I'll have to adjust his seat, at the lunch break."

One of the guides cycles up beside her. His name is Paolo, he tells her. He asks if that is her son at the front? "*Sì,*" she says.

"*Permesso,*" he asks, respectfully, as he places his arm around her waist, pulls her cycle toward his own, and locks her in a form of embrace, their legs pumping in unison, his breath in her ear. He tells her gently, "*Si soffre meno vicino a quelli davanti al gruppo.*" You will suffer less near the front of the group. "*Fidati di me. E potrai anche guardare tuo figlio.*" Paolo must have a minor in psychology, as the ability to watch her son is definitely persuasive. Francesca lowers her head, relaxes her entire body to the point of closing her eyes, and lets Paolo pedal for them both. An amazing stillness enters upon her. She listens to his breathing, to the sound of the Sardegnan wind. When she opens her eyes she notices that Paolo has the most powerful quads she has ever seen. Robert calls out to her, with the insulation of language: "We're all jealous, Francesca. Give into it."

Paolo speaks quietly to the cyclists as he moves her seamlessly forward into the group, telling each man, by name, to give way, jockeys her toward the middle, behind the front flank, three rows behind her son. Suddenly, he releases her, and there is wind beneath her. She flies, as if without effort. Uncomprehending. How did the obstruction lift, the wall that had kept her from this? Paolo is true to his word. She suffers less in this position – drafted by the strongest, those in front of the group, who take the wind on their chests.

Francesca looks around herself in amazement.

"*Sei brava, Signora,*" an old man says to her, *sotto voce,* just off to her right. She glances sideways at his face, at its wrinkles. Yet here, where they are, old as he must be, the man appears to have no trouble keeping up. *Why does he whisper,* she wonders.

"*È vero?*" she whispers back.

"*Sì, è vero,*" he whispers again, as if what he is about to say next must remain their secret, "*Hai coraggio.*"

Francesca rides like this for at least another half hour. She is euphoric. She takes the old man's blessing. She takes the wind. She takes Paolo's rescue and Paolo's release. She takes joy in the Sardegnan landscape, joy in celebrating her son's backside.

Her son, in the lead, has no idea whatsoever what has become of his mother. Knowing Marco, she also knows he will be worried. *C'mon* she thinks, *let's have fun with this.*

They are close to the town where they will stop for refreshments before turning back. Francesca books it out to the left, to the mid-point of the road. Then, lifting up from the bike seat, she puts all she has into the homestretch. Excitement rises behind her.

Vada, signora, vada, vada…

The ripple of voices rise like a wave. The men at the front have no idea what is happening, *Vada, signora, vada!*....

Francesca whizzes past. As she does so, she breaks into song: *"We are the champions, we are the champions..."* – which she and her son used to sing at the top of their lungs driving across country, the car stereo blaring – glancing toward the right, to catch the vision of her son's "fish" look of amazement. ...*where in hell did she come from?*

Grazie, Francesca thinks. *Grazie, grazie...*

And so they enter the town, with Francesca riding a wave of euphoria, laughing as she dismounts her bike and into the arms of Dominique who, unaccountably, is weeping, and her son, who keeps asking her over and over again, "Are you riding back? Are you riding it back?"

"Of course I'm riding back. The way through is the way back. There's only one way back..."

"So what do you mean, I go for tarts?"

They are at the Rome airport, four hours of wait time before boarding the flight that will take them home.

"Do you think Emma is a tart?"

"No…" The unspoken *but* hovers in the air between them. And then Marco asks the question that is worth the whole of their Sardegna.

"So what *really* do you think of Emma?"

Francesca doesn't hesitate.

"People fall into patterns, and this is Emma's pattern… It is not *if* Emma is going to break your heart again, but *when* and how badly it's going to hurt this time."

Because, my son,
La bella Cristina to whom you give your love
Must treasure you,
As you do her,
As I do you—
As your father didn't me,
My one, only son,
Whether she have the body of a goddess, or
Face of a dog.

Her first bicycle had been blue, with cream-coloured fenders, chrome handlebars, and blue-and-white streamers – one speed, with a bell. Every time Francesca's foot had touched the pedal she'd gone off into her own adventure, face to the wind, home at her back. Over the years, the seat and handlebars had got adjusted upward. The bike had lost a spoke, never to be replaced. When she had gone to law school, her father had painted it and added a basket, for the groceries she purchased weekly at Ferlisi Brothers. She had kept it in the hallway of her campus apartment. Then it had sat in the shed of her first home. She'd wept inconsolably at learning her husband, Marco's father, had sold it without asking permission. That bike had meant the world to her. It had been the world. On it, everything had been possible and she had been all she could be – setting the sidewalks ablaze.

It got you there, her father says, in defence of the old bike, when Francesca tells him this story to help pass the time. Francesca's father is hooked up to his dialysis machine, and accepting, she thinks, of whatever is left of his journey. He has achieved the age of ninety-three.

More than there, Francesca suggests. Where is there, anyway?

There is not a place. Not a destination.

There is the journey.

"You can make it, sweet pea, yes you can… Momma's here…" And there she was, and is to this day, on her knees, praying for his journey, at the end of the long hallway, her arms outstretched, watching her son crawl toward her on all fours, pausing to understand the

distance between himself and his mother, no concept as yet of time, the distance down the long dark corridor in the old house on Glebeholme Avenue – his face open – as yet without suffering, not even the suffering of birth, as he has been delivered by caesarean section. And when he reaches his destination, she sweeps him into her arms and, unaccountably, weeps and laughs, joyful at his accomplishment. Their accomplishment. For this is huge. Her son's first journey… the one down the hallway of their first home, toward the destination of mother, who waits for him still, letting him seek and find, all on his own.

She knows this moment has to be, just as she knows he cannot stay in the same place forever. Yet she knows she somehow will also always be there, in that place, in the hallway, on Glebeholme Avenue.

"It is a good thing we didn't know," her son says of the *giro* years later. Francesca is describing how for months afterward, and even now, she will think of a particularly dangerous bend where her bike had wobbled and the voices of alarmed men had gone up all around her, the prospect of the tumble of bikes and bodies that could have happened. "It's a good thing we didn't know what we were getting into. We just put our feet to the pedal, and went."

ACKNOWLEDGMENTS

"Vivi's Florentine Scarf" won the 2002 Paolucci Prize of the American-Italian Writers Association, and was then published in *Joy, Joy, Why Do I Sing?* Women's Press, an imprint of Canadian Scholars' Press Inc.: Toronto, 2004.

"Afternoon in a Garden of the Palazzo Barberini," *Accenti Magazine*, Winter, 2010, reprinted in *Reflections on Culture, An Anthology of Creative and Critical Writing,* the Frank Iacobucci Centre for Italian Canadian Studies, 2010.

"Waiting" was originally published in *Bottled Roses,* Oberon, 1985, then in *Joy, Joy, Why Do I Sing?* Women's Press, an imprint of Canadian Scholars' Press Inc.: Toronto, 2004. An expanded version appeared in *ELQ (Exile: the Literary Quarterly) Magazine,* Volume 36, No.1, 2012. The story was shortlisted for the Vanderbilt/Exile Short Fiction Competiton 2011-12, and that version appeared in the subsequent publication of the *Carter V. Cooper Short Fiction Anthology*, Book Two.

"Getting Off So Lightly" was originally published in *Joy, Joy, Why Do I Sing?* Women's Press, an imprint of Canadian Scholars' Press Inc.: Toronto, 2004.

"Powerful Novena of Childlike Confidence," originally published in *Making Olives and Other Family Secrets*, Longbridge Books: Montreal, Spring, 2008.

"Entering Sicily" was originally published in a special edition of *Descant: Sicily, Land of Forgotten Dreams*, Vol. 154, Fall, 2011.

"Travel Stories" was originally published in *ELQ (Exile: the Literary Quarterly) Magazine*, Volume 31, No.1, 2007.

Scan for the author speaking about the competition, or URL:
www.tinyurl.com/Madott-VanderbiltCompetitions

RECYCLED
Paper made from
recycled material
FSC® C100212